I0542293

The Pony Rider Boys In Montana

Frank Gee Patchin

1st WORLD
LIBRARY
Literary Society

The Pony Rider Boys in Montana

Frank Gee Patchin

© 1st World Library – Literary Society, 2005
PO Box 2211
Fairfield, IA 52556
www.1stworldlibrary.org
First Edition

LCCN: 2006902694

Softcover ISBN: 1-4218-1827-2
Hardcover ISBN: 1-4218-1727-6
eBook ISBN: 1-4218-1927-9

Purchase *"The Pony Rider Boys in Montana"*
as a traditional bound book at:
www.1stWorldLibrary.org/purchase.asp?ISBN=1-4218-1827-2

1st World Library Literary Society is a nonprofit
organization dedicated to promoting literacy by:

- Creating a free internet library accessible from any computer worldwide.
- Hosting writing competitions and offering book publishing scholarships.

Readers interested in supporting literacy
through sponsorship, donations or
membership please contact:
literacy@1stworldlibrary.org
Check us out at: www.1stworldlibrary.ORG
and start downloading free ebooks today.

The Pony Rider Boys in Montana
contributed by Tim, Ed & Rodney
in support of
1st World Library Literary Society

CONTENTS

CHAPTER I

FITTING OUT FOR THE JOURNEY

"Forsythe!" announced the trainman in a loud voice.

"That is where we get off, is it not!" asked Tad Butler.

"Yes, this is the place," answered Professor Zepplin.

"I don't see any place," objected Stacy Brown, peering from the car window. "Where is it?"

"You'll see it in a minute," said Walter Perkins.

"Chunky, we are too busy to bother answering all your silly questions. Why don't you get a railroad guide? Town's on the other side. It's one of those one-sided towns. Use your eyes more and your tongue less," added Ned Rector impatiently.

With this injunction, Ned rose and began pulling his belongings from the rack over his head, which action was followed by the three other boys in the party. Professor Zepplin had already risen and was walking toward the car door.

The Northern Pacific train on which they were riding, came to a slow, noisy stop. From it, alighted the four boys, sun-burned, clear-eyed and springy of step. They were clad in the regulation suits of the cowboy, the faded garments giving evidence of long service on the open plains.

Accompanying the lads was a tall, athletic looking man, his face deeply bronzed from exposure to wind, sun and storm, his iron gray beard standing out in strong contrast, giving to his sun burned features a ferocious appearance that was not at all in keeping with the man's real nature.

A man dressed in a neat business suit, but wearing a broad brimmed sombrero stepped up to the boys without the least hesitation, the moment they reached the platform.

"Are you the Pony Rider Boys?" he asked smilingly.

"We are, sir," replied Tad, lifting his hat courteously.

"Glad to know you, young man. I am Mr. Simms the banker here. I was requested by banker Perkins of Chillicothe, Missouri, to meet you young gentlemen. Funds for your use while here are deposited in my bank ready for your order. Where is Professor - Professor -"

"Zepplin?"

"Yes, that's the name." "This is he," Tad informed him, introducing the Professor.

"If you and the young men will come up to the bank we will talk matters over. I would ask you to my house, but my family is spending the summer at my ranch out near Gracy Butte."

"It is just as well," said the Professor. "We are not exactly up here on a social mission. The boys are crowding all the time possible into their life during their vacation. I presume they are anxious to get started again."

Leaving their baggage at the railroad station, the party set off up the street with the banker, to make final arrangements for the journey to which they looked forward with keen anticipation.

Readers of this series will remember how, in "THE PONY RIDER BOYS IN THE ROCKIES," the four lads set off on horseback to spend part of their summer vacation in the mountains. The readers will remember too, the many thrilling experiences that the boys passed through on that eventful trip, between hunting big game in hand to hand conflict, fighting a real battle with the bad men of the mountains, and how in the end they discovered and took possession of the Lost Claim.

Readers will also remember how the lads next joined in a cattle drive, and their adventures and exciting trip across the plains in "THE PONY RIDER BOYS IN TEXAS."

It will be recalled that on this expedition they became cowboys in reality, living the life of the cattle men, sharing their duties and their hardships, participating in wild, daring night rides, facing appalling storms, battling with swollen torrents, bravely facing many perils, and tow eventually Tad Butler and his companions solved the Veiled Riddle of the Plains, thus bringing great happiness to others as well as keen satisfaction to themselves.

After having completed their eventful trip in Texas, the boys had expressed a desire to next make a trip of exploration to the north country. Arrangements had therefore been made by the father of Walter Perkins for a journey into the wilder parts of Montana.

None of the details, however, had been decided upon. The boys felt that they were now experienced enough to be allowed to make their own arrangements, always, of course, with the approval of their companion, Professor Zepplin.

As a result they arrived in Forsythe one hot July day, about noon. Their ponies had been shipped home, the little fellows having become a bit too docile to suit the tastes of the lads, who had been riding bucking bronchos during their trip on a cattle drive in southern Texas. They knew they would have little difficulty in finding animals to suit them up in the grazing country.

"And now what are your plans, young men?" smiled the hanker, after all had taken seats in his office in the rear of the bank.

The lads waited for Professor Zepplin to speak.

"Tell Mr. Simms what you have in mind," he urged.

"We had thought of going over the old Custer trail," spoke up Walter.

"Where, down in the Black Hills?"

"No, not so far down as that. We should like to go over

the trail he followed and visit the scene of his last battle and get a little mountain trip as well -- "

"Are there any mountains around here?" asked Stacy innocently.

Mr. Simms laughed, in which he was joined by the boys.

"My lad, there's not much else up here. You'll find all the mountains you want and some that you will not want -- "

"Any Indians?" asked Chunky.

"State's full of them."

"Good Indians, of course," nodded the Professor.

"Well, you know the old saying that 'the only good Indian is a dead Indian.' They're good when they have to be. We have very little trouble with the Crows, but sometimes the Black feet and Flat Heads get off their reservations and cause us a little trouble."

Chunky was listening with wide open eyes. "I - I don't like Indians," he stammered. "None of us are overfond of them, I guess. Since you arrived I have been thinking of something that may interest you."

"We are in your hands," smiled the Professor.

"As I said a short time ago, I have a ranch out near Gracy Butte."

"Cattle?" asked Tad, with quickened interest.

"No, sheep. I have another up on the Missouri River. I am getting in five thousand more sheep that some of my men are bringing in on a drive. They should be along very shortly now."

"You deal in large numbers in this country," smiled the Professor.

"Yes, we have to if we expect to make a profit. I intend to send these five thousand new sheep to the Missouri River ranch. It will be a long, hard drive and we shall need some extra men. How would you boys like to join the outfit and go through with them? I promise you you will get all the outdoor life you want."

"Well, I don't know," said Tad doubtfully. "I don't just like sheep."

Mr. Simms laughed.

"You've been with a cattle outfit. I can see that. You have learned to hate sheep and for no reason - no good reason whatever. Sheep are a real pleasure to manage. Besides, they are wholesome, intelligent little animals. The cattle men resent their being on the range for the reason that the sheep crop down the grass so close that the cattle are unable to get enough. They try to drive us off."

"By what right?" interrupted the Professor.

"Right of strength, that's all. On free grass we have as much right as the cattle men. Have you your own ponies?"

"No; we expect to purchase some here. Can you

recommend us to a ranch where we can fit ourselves out? We have our saddles and camp outfit, of course," said Tad.

"Yes; I'll take you out to my brother's ranch just outside the town. He has some lively little bronchos there. He won't ask you any fancy price, either. If you buy, why, you can give him an order on my bank and I will settle with him. You know you have funds here for your requirements. What do you say to the sheep idea?"

"Will you let us think it over, Mr. Simms!" asked Walter.

"Why, certainly. You will have plenty of time to visit the Rosebud Mountains as well. I have arranged for a guide. You will find him at the edge of the foothills where he lives. You can't miss him. When do you plan to start?" asked the banker.

"We thought we should like to get away today," replied Tad.

"I see you are not losing any time, young men. We may be able to fix you up so you can start this afternoon. You will want to camp out, I imagine, and not make the journey in one day."

"Oh, yes, we are used to that," interjected Ned. "We have slept out of doors so long now that we should not feel comfortable in a real bed."

"I understand. I have been a cowboy as well as sheep-man, and have spent many weeks on the open range. It was different then," he added reminiscently. "We will drive out to my brother's ranch now, if you are ready."

The boys rose instantly. They were looking forward to having their new ponies, with keen anticipation.

After a short drive they reached the ranch, and a herd of half wild ponies was driven into a corral where the lads might look them over and make their choice.

"I think that little bay there, with the pink eyes "will suit me," decided Tad. "Is he saddle broken?"

"After a fashion, yes. He's been out a few times. But he's full of ginger," announced the cowboy who was showing the horses to them.

"That's what I want. Don't like to have to use the spur to keep my mount from going to sleep," laughed the boy.

"You won't need the irons to keep this pony awake or yerself either."

"You may give me the most gentle beast on the premises," spoke up the Professor. "I have had quite enough of wild horses and their pranks," a speech at which the boys all laughed heartily.

"Me too," agreed Chunky.

"You'll take what you get. You couldn't stay on any kind of horse for long at a time. Why, you'd fall off one of those wooden horses that they have in harness shops," announced Ned Rector witheringly.

"I can ride as well as you can," retorted the fat boy,

looking his tormentor straight in the eyes.

"Chunky means business when he looks at you that way," laughed Walter. "Better keep away from him, Ned."

"Think I'll take the pink-eyed one," decided Tad. "Pink-eye. That will be a good name for him. Got a rope?"

"Yes, kin you rope him?"

"I'll try if you will stir them up a bit," answered the freckle-faced boy.

"You might as well pick out our ponies, too," observed the Professor. "You are the only one of our party who is a competent judge of horse flesh."

Tad nodded. His rope was held loosely in his hand, the broad loop lying on the ground a few feet behind him, while the cowboy began milling the biting, kicking animals about the corral.

Now Pink-eye's head was raised above the back of his fellows so that Tad got a good roping sight. The lariat began curving in the air, then its great loop opened, shot out and dropped neatly over the head of the pink-eyed pony. Tad drew it taut before it settled to the animal's shoulder, at the same time throwing his full weight on the rawhide.

He would have been equally successful in trying to hold a steam engine. Before the lad had time to swing the line and throw the pony from its feet, the muscular little animal had leaped to one side.

The sudden jerk hurled the boy through the air.

"Look out!" warned the cowboy.

His warning came too late.

Tad was thrown with great force full against the heels of another broncho.

"He'll be killed!" cried Professor Zepplin.

Up went the pony's hind feet and with them Tad Butler. The pony came down as quickly as it had gone up, but Tap kept on going. He had been near the wire corral when he was jerked against the animal's feet.

The pony kicked a clean goal and Tad was projected over the wire fence, landing in a heap several feet outside the corral.

The lad was on his feet almost instantly. When they saw that be had not been seriously injured the boys set up a defiant yell.

"Hurt you any?" grinned the cowboy.

"Only my pride," answered Tad, with a sheepish smile. "I never had that happen to me before."

"Other ponies got in your way so you couldn't throw your rope down on the pink-eyed one and trip him. I'll get him out for you."

"You will do nothing of the sort. I can rope my own stock."

After having obtained another lariat, Tad, not deeming it wise to attempt to try to pick up the rope that the animal was dragging about the corral, once more took his station, while the cowman began milling them around the enclosure by sundry shouts and prods.

There was much kicking and squealing.

"Now cut him out!" shouted Tad.

The cowboy did so. Pink-eye was beating a tattoo in the air with his heels. He was occupying a little open space all by himself at that moment.

The rope again curled through the air. Tad gave it a quick undulating motion after feeling the pull on the pony's neck, and the next moment the little animal fell heavily to his side.

"Woof!" said the pony.

"Come out of here!" commanded the lad, jerking the animal to its feet and starting for the exit.

The pink-eyed broncho followed its new master out as if he had been doing so every day for a long time.

Tad picked out a spotted roan for Stacy Brown, to which he gave the appropriate name of "Painted-squaw". Bad-eye, was considered an appropriate name for Ned Rector's broncho, while Walter drew a dapple gray which he decided to call Buster.

After choosing a well broken animal for the Professor, and picking out a suitable pack horse, the boys announced that they were ready for the start. An hour or so was spent in getting provisions enough to last them for a few days, all of which, together with their camp equipment, was strapped to the backs of the ponies.

It was now three o'clock in the afternoon. Ahead of them was a thirty mile journey over an unknown trail.

"I think we had better have a guide to take us out to the foothills until we shall have found our permanent guide," said the Professor.

"No, please don't," urged Tad.

"We are plainsmen enough now to he able to find our own way," added Ned. "It's a clear trail. We can see the Rosebud Range from here. That's it over there, isn't it, Mr. Simms?"

"Yes," replied the banker. "All you will have to do will be to get your direction by your compass before you start, and hold to it. You will not be able to see the mountains all the time, as the country is rolling and there are numerous buttes between here and there."

"Any Indians?" asked Stacy apprehensively.

"You may see some, but they will not bother you," laughed the banker. "I shall hope to have you all spend next Sunday with us at my ranch; then we can discuss our plans for your joining my outfit."

"How far is it from where we are bound?" asked the Professor.

"Not more than twenty miles. Just a few hours' ride."

Filled with joyful anticipations the little party set out, headed for the mountain ranges that lay low in the southwest, some thirty miles distant. Contrary to their usual practice, they had taken no cook with them, having decided to rely wholly on their own resources for a time at least, which they felt themselves safe in doing after their many experiences thus far on their summer vacation.

The little western village was soon left behind them. Turning in their saddles, they found that it had sunk out of sight. They could not tell behind which of the endless succession of high and low buttes the town was nestling. Tad consulted his compass, after which the lads faced the southwest and pressed cheerfully on.

The Pony Rider Boys were fairly started now on what was to prove the most exciting and eventful journey of their lives.

CHAPTER II

YAWNS PROVE DISASTROUS

"Yah-h-h hum." Stacy Brown yawned loudly. "Yah-hum," breathed Walter Perkins, half rousing himself from his nap.

"Ho-ho-hum," added the deep bass voice of Professor Zepplin.

"Yah - see here, stop that!" commanded Ned Rector, suddenly raising himself to a sitting posture. "You've done nothing but stretch your mouth in yawns ever since we reached Montana. See, you've waked up the whole camp."

"Ho-hum," said Chunky.

"Say, what ails you?" demanded Tad, putting down by supreme force of will, his own inclination to yawn.

"I - I guess - yah - it must be the - the mountain air. Yah-hum," yawned the fat boy.

Pink-eye coughed off among the cedars.

"What means all this disturbance, young gentlemen?" demanded the Professor.

"It's Chunky and the bronchos yawning," Ned Rector informed him.

"So did you," observed Stacy Brown.

"Did what?"

"Yawned. See, see! Your mouth's open now. You're going to yawn this very second You -- "

His taunts were lost in the shouts of the Pony Riders. Ned Rector's face was set determinedly, a vacant expression having taken full possession of his eyes.

"He is going to yawn," announced Walter solemnly. "Stake down the camp."

In spite of his determination not to yield to the impulse of the moment, Ned's mouth slowly opened to its extreme capacity, accompanied by a deep intake of breath.

"Y-a-h-h-h-hum!" he exploded.

"Got you that time. He - he -- " Walter's words died away in a long-drawn, gaping yawn.

Ned waited to hear no more. With a yell he projected himself at the fat boy. Stacy, however, observing the move, had quickly rolled to one side. Ned struck the ground heavily.

Stacy was rolling over and over now as if his very life depended upon getting away. He could not spare the time to get up and run, so he continued to roll over and over, making no mean progress at that.

"Go it, Chunky!" shouted Walter in high glee.

The scene, dimly lighted by the smouldering camp-fire, was so ludicrous as to send the boys into shouts of laughter. All were thoroughly awake now. They had made camp at sunset on the banks of the East Fork, of what was known as Fennell's Creek, a broad, deep stream which, joining its companion fork some ten miles further down, flowed into the clear waters of the Yellowstone. Here they had cooked their supper after many attempts, made with varying degrees of success and much laughter. Later they had rolled themselves into their blankets and gone to sleep.

They had been awakened by Stacy Brown's yawns. In a moment each had taken his turn at yawning, but all took the interruption good-naturedly, save Ned Rector. By this time he had grown very much excited. No sooner would he pounce upon the spot where Stacy appeared to be, than the fat boy by a few swift rolls would propel himself well beyond the reach of his irate companion.

"It'll be the worse for you when I do get you," cried Ned.

At that moment Ned tripped over a limb, and, plunging headlong, measured his length on the ground.

The sympathy of the camp was with the rolling Chunky.

"Get a net," shouted Walter.

"No, rope him, Ned. That's the only way you ever will catch him," jeered Tad.

Both boys were dancing about their companions, shivering in their pajamas and uttering shouts of glee.

"He's a regular high roller," said Tad.

"No, not a high roller," answered Walter.

"Here, here!" admonished the Professor. "Stop this nonsense. I want to go to sleep. I don't mind you young gentlemen enjoying yourselves, but midnight is rather late for such pranks, it strikes me. Into your blankets, every one of you."

It was doubtful that the boys even heard his voice. If they did, they failed entirely to catch the meaning of his words, so absorbed were they in the mad scramble of Ned Rector and Stacy Brown.

"Roll, Chunky, roll!" urged Walter, jumping up and down in his bare feet.

"Good thing he's fat. If he weren't so round he could never do it," mocked Tad. "I'll bet he was a fast creeper when be was a baby."

The ponies, disturbed by the noise and excitement, had scrambled to their feet and were moving about restlessly in the bushes where they were tethered.

"Master Stacy, you will get up at once!" commanded the Professor sternly.

"I can't," wailed the fat boy.

"Then I'll help you," decided the Professor firmly, striding toward the spot where he had last heard the lad's voice.

"Look out for the river!" warned Tad, as the thought of what was below the boy suddenly occurred to him.

"Help, help! I'm rolling in," cried Stacy.

"There he goes, down the bank! Grab him!" shouted Walter.

"Where?" demanded Ned, not fully grasping the import of the warning.

"There, there! Don't you see him? Right in front of you. He's going to fall into the river!"

Stacy had forgotten that they were encamped on the east shore of the fork and that the broad stream was flowing rapidly along just below him. The banks at that point were high and precipitous, the water almost icy cold, being fresh from the clear mountain streams a few miles above. In spots it was deep and treacherous.

Frantically grasping at weeds and slender sprouts, as he rolled down the almost perpendicular bluff, Stacy yelled lustily for help. From the soft, sandy soil the weeds came away in his hands, without in the slightest degree checking his progress.

Tad realized the danger perhaps more fully than did the others. In the darkness the lad might slip into one of the treacherous river pockets and drown before they could reach him.

Grasping his rope which lay beside his cot. Tad sprang to the top of the bluff, swinging the loop of his lariat above his head as he ran.

He could faintly make out the figure of his companion rolling down the steep bank.

"Hold up your hand so I can drop the rope over you," shouted Tad, at the same time making a skillful cast.

His aim was true. The rawhide reached the mark. Chunky, however, feeling it slap him smartly on the cheek, brushed the rope aside in his excitement, not realizing what it was that had struck him.

"Grab it!" roared Tad, observing that he had failed to rope the lad.

With a mighty splash, Stacy Brown plunged into the stream broadside on.

"He's in! I heard him strike!" cried Walter.

With a warning cry to the others to bring lights, Tad, without an instant's hesitation, leaped over the bluff and went shooting down it in a sitting posture.

"Tad's gone in, too," shouted Walter excitedly, as their ears caught a second splash. It was more clean cut than had been Stacy's dive, and might have passed unnoticed had they not known the meaning of the sound.

Ned Rector stood as if dazed. He knew that somehow he had thoughtlessly plunged his companions into dire peril.

"Wha - what is it?" he stammered.

"They're in the river! Don't you understand?" answered Walter sharply, moving forward as if to follow over the bank in an effort to rescue his companion.

"Keep back!" commanded the Professor. "You'll all drown if you go over that bank."

The Professor, with more presence of mind than the others, had sprung up and rushed for the camp-fire, from which he snatched a burning ember.

At any other time the sight of his long, gaunt figure, clad in a full suit of pink pajamas, dashing madly about the camp, would have excited the lads to uproarious merriment. But laughter was far from their thoughts at that moment.

"Use your eyes! Do you see him?" demanded Professor Zepplin, peering down anxiously into the shadows.

"No. Oh, Tad!" shouted Ned. There was no reply to the boy's hail. "Thaddeus!" roared the Professor. Still no answer.

Down the stream a short distance they could hear the water roaring over the rocks, from where it dropped some twenty feet and continued on its course. The falls there were known as Buttermilk Falls, because of the churning the water received in its lively drop, and more than one mountaineer had been swept over them to his death in times of high water. Between the camp and these falls there was a sharp bend in the river, and ere the boys had recovered from their surprise, their companions undoubtedly had been swept around the bend and on beyond their sight.

"Do - do you - do you think -- " stammered Walter.

"They have gone down stream," answered the Professor shortly. "Run for it, boys! Run as you never ran before!"

Ned dived for the thicket where the ponies were tethered. It was the work of a moment only to release Bad-eye. Without waiting to saddle him, Ned threw himself upon the surprised animal's back, and with a wild yell sent the broncho plunging through the camp.

He was nearly unseated when Bad-eye suddenly veered to avoid stepping into the camp-fire, which Ned Rector in his haste had forgotten.

The lad gripped the pony's mane and hung on desperately until he finally succeeded in righting himself, all the while kicking the pony's sides with his bare feet to urge him on faster.

They were out of the camp, tearing through the thicket before the Professor and Walter had even gotten beyond the glow of the fire. Ned was obliged to make a wide detour instead of taking a short cut across the bend made by the river. There were rocks in his way, so that a few moments of valuable time were lost before he reached the stream on the other side of the obstruction.

"Come, we must run," urged the Professor. "I'm afraid both of them may have gone over the falls."

"Oh, I hope he is not too late!" answered Walter, with a half sob, as they ran regardless of the fact that sharp sticks and jagged stones were cruelly cutting into their feet.

CHAPTER III

THE BOYS RESCUE EACH OTHER

Ned swung around the bend at a tremendous pace. He was able to see little about him, though as he once more reached the bank he could tell where the river lay, because the river gorge lay in a deeper shadow than did the rest of the landscape about him.

"Oh, Tad! Tad!" he shouted.

A faint call answered him. He was not quite sure that it was not an echo of his own voice.

"Tad! T-a-d!"

"Hurry!"

It seemed a long distance away - that faint reply to his hail.

"That you, Tad!"

"Y-e-s."

"Where are you!"

"Here."

"Where? I don't see you."

"In the river. Just below the bend."

Hurriedly dismounting and making a quick examination of the banks he discovered that they were so nearly straight up and down that it would be impossible to get his companions out at that point.

"I can't get you out here. You'll have to wait a few moments. Are you swimming?"

"No, I am holding to a rock. It's awful slippery and I'm freezing too."

"All right. Is Stacy with you?"

"Yes, I've got him. "

"Good! Have courage! I'll be with you," said Ned encouragingly.

"You'll have to hurry. I can't hold on much longer. The falls are just below here and if I have to let go it's all up with us."

Ned had no need to be told that. He could almost feel the spray from the falls on his face, so close were they to him and their roar was loud in his ears, so that he was obliged to raise his voice in calling to his companions.

Leaping to the back of Bad-eye, Ned was off like a shot, tearing through the brush, headed toward camp. On the way he passed Professor Zepplin and Walter, nearly running them down in his mad haste.

"Got a rope?" he shouted in passing. "No," answered Walter. "Then get one and hurry around the bend. You'll be needed there in a minute. I'm going down into the stream from the camp."

The Professor, seeming to comprehend what Ned had in mind, turned and ran back to the camp.

Without an instant's hesitation, Ned Rector, upon reaching their camping place, put his pony at the bank where the two boys had gone over.

The little animal refused to take it. He bucked and the lad had a narrow escape from following where Tad and Chunky had gone a short time before.

"I've got to have a saddle. That's the only way I can stick on to drive him in, and we'll need it to hold to as well," he decided.

Every moment was precious now. Whirling the animal about, Ned drove him into the thicket where the saddles lay folded against trees.

It was the work of seconds for him to leap off and throw the heavy saddle on Bad-eye's back. The boy worked with the speed and precision of a Gattling gun. Yet he groaned hopelessly when he realized that his delay might mean the death of two of his companions.

Professor Zepplin arrived at the camp just as Ned had finally cinched the girths and swung himself into the saddle.

"Where - where is he?" gasped the Professor, now breathing hard.

"Below the bend. Get back there with a rope and be ready to toss it to him if he lets go."

Ned and his pony crashed through the brush. He had no spur with which to urge on the animal, but Ned had thoughtfully picked up a long, stout stick, and once more they drove straight at the high bank.

"Stop! I forbid it!" thundered the Professor.

Ned paid no more attention to him than had he not spoken. It was a time when words were useless. What was necessary was action and quick action at that.

"Hurry with that rope!" commanded Ned.

The pony slowed up as they approached the bank of the river, but Ned was in no mood for trifling now. He brought down the stick on the animal's hip with a terrific whack.

Bad-eye angered by the blow, squealed and leaped into the air with all four feet free of the ground.

"Hi-yi!" exclaimed the Pony Rider sharply, again smiting the animal while the latter was still in the air.

Ned's plan was to enter the stream at that point and swim down with the pony until they should have reached the boys and rescued them from their perilous position. While the bluff was sandy at the point where they had fallen in, down below, where Tad was now desperately clinging to the rock, the stream wound through a rocky cut, whose high sides were slippery and uncertain, especially in the darkness of the night.

Bad-eye needed no further goading to force him to do his master's bidding. With another squeal of protest the little animal plunged for the bank. No sooner had his forward feet reached over the edge of it than the treacherous sands gave way beneath them.

The pony pivoted on its head, landing violently on its back. Ned had dismounted without the least effort on his part, so that he was well out of the way when his mount landed. He had been hurled from the saddle the instant the pony's feet struck the unresisting sand.

But Ned clung doggedly to the bridle reins. He, too, struck on his back. He heard the squealing, kicking pony floundering down upon him, its every effort to right itself forcing it further and further down the slippery bank. Now on its back, now with its nose in the sand, Bad-eye was rapidly nearing the swiftly moving creek. Ned had all he could do to keep out of the way, and on account of the darkness he had to be guided more by instinct than by any other sense. However, it was not difficult to keep track of the now thoroughly frightened animal.

Ned leaped to one side. An instant later, and he would have been caught under the pony.

The animal hit the water with a mighty splash, with Ned still clinging to the reins. As the pony went in, Ned was jerked in also, striking the water head first.

He could have screamed from the shock of the icy water, which seemed to smite him like a heavy blow.

For a moment boy and pony floundered about in the stream. It seemed almost a miracle that the lad was not killed by those flying hoofs that were beating the water almost into a froth.

As soon as he was able to get to the surface Ned exerted all his strength to swim out further toward the middle of the stream. Even when he was under water, he still kept a firm grip on the rein. To let go would be to lose all that he had gained after so much danger in getting as far as he had.

By this time, both boy and pony had drifted down stream several rods.

The pony righted himself and struck out for the bank. Ned was by his side almost instantly, being aided in the effort to get there by having the reins to pull himself in by.

Bad-eye refused instinctively to head down stream. There was only one thing to do. That was to climb into the saddle and get him started. Ned did this with difficulty. His weight made the pony sink at first, the animal whinnying with fear.

Fearing to drown the broncho, the boy slipped off, at the same time taking a firm grip on the lines.

Bad-eye came to the surface at once. Ned's right hand was on the pommel, the reins bunched in his left. He brought his knee sharply against the animal's side.

"Whoop!" he urged, again driving the knee against the pony's ribs.

Under the strong guiding hand of his master, the animal fighting every inch of the way, began swimming down stream.

"I'm coming!" shouted the boy.

Before that moment he had not had breath nor the time to call.

"I'm coming!" he repeated, as they swung around the wide sweeping curve.

"Are you there, Tad?"

"Yes," was the scarcely distinguishable reply. "I've got to let go."

"You hold on. Bad-eye and I will be there in a minute and the Professor is hurrying down along the bank with a rope."

"I'm freezing. I'm all numb, that's the trouble," answered Tad weakly.

Ned knew that the plucky lad was well-nigh exhausted. The strain of holding to the slippery rock in the face of the swift current was one that would have taxed the strength of the strongest man, to say nothing of the almost freezing cold water, which chilled the blood and benumbed the senses.

"You've gone past me," cried Tad.

"I know it. I'm heading up," replied Ned Rector.

Ned had purposely driven his pony further down stream so that he might the easier pick them up as he went by on the return trip.

"Are you all right down there?" called the Professor, who had reached a point on the bank opposite to them.

"Yes, but get ready to cast me a rope," directed Ned.

"I'm afraid I cannot."

"Then have Walter do it."

"He is not here. I directed him to remain in camp in case he was needed there."

"All right. You can try later. I'll tell you how. I'm busy now."

"Don't run me down," warned Tad Butler.

"Keep talking then, so I'll know where you are. Just say yip-yip and keep it up."

Tad did so, but his voice was weak and uncertain.

Ned swam the pony alongside of them, pulling hard on the reins to slow the animal down without exerting pressure enough to stop him.

"Is Chunky able to help himself?"

"Yes, if he will."

"Then both of you grab Bad-eye by the mane as he goes by. Don't you miss, for if you do, we're all lost."

"The pony won't be able to get the three of us up the stream," objected Tad.

"I know it."

"Then, what are we going to do?"

"I'll stay here and hang on. You send Walter back with the pony as soon as you get there. Better call to him to get Pink-eye or one of the others saddled as soon as you can make him hear. We'll save time that way. I'm afraid Bad-eye won't be able to make the return trip."

"Now grab for the rock," cried Tad.

Ned did so, but he missed it.

Tad still clinging to Chunky fastened his right hand in the broncho's mane. All three of the boys were now clinging to the overburdened animal. Ned began swimming to assist the pony, for he realized that they had dropped back a few feet in taking on the extra weight.

"Work further back and get hold of the saddle," Ned directed.

Tad followed his instructions.

"I'm afraid he'll never make it," groaned Ned. "I -- "

At that instant his hand came in violent contact with a hard, cold object. It was the slender, pillar-like rock that Tad had been clinging to for so long in the icy water.

"I've got it," exclaimed Ned.

He cast loose from Bad-eye and threw both arms about the rock. The pony freed from a share of his burden, struck off up stream against the current, making excellent headway.

"I don't like to do this," Tad called back. "I wouldn't, were it not for Chunky. He couldn't have stood it there another minute."

"You can't help yourself now. How's the kid?" called Ned.

"He's all right now."

"Professor, are you up there?"

"Yes."

He had heard the dialogue between the boys, and understood well what had been done.

"That was a brave thing to do, Master Ned."

"Thank you, Professor. Suppose you try to cast that rope to me. I'm afraid I shall never be able to hold on here alone as long as Tad did. B-r-r-r, but it's cold!" he shivered.

The Professor tried his hand at casting the lariat.

"Never touched me," said Ned, more to keep up his own spirits than with the intent to speak slightingly of the Professor's effort.

"Take it up stream throw it out, then let it float down," suggested Ned.

Professor Zepplin did so, but the rope was found to be

too short to reach, and at Ned's direction, he made no further attempt.

Soon Ned heard some one shouting cheerily up the stream. It was Tad Butler. He had dashed up to camp immediately upon reaching shore, and the exercise restored his circulation. Walter, who was in camp had Pink-eye ready and saddled for an emergency, and Tad mounting the pony, forced him to take to the water. He was now returning to rescue his brave friend, who was clinging to the rock. He had been unwilling to trust the perilous trip to anyone else.

"I was afraid Walt would go over the falls, pony and all," he explained, wheeling alongside Ned Rector and picking him up from the rock.

"I'll run a foot race with you when we get ashore," laughed Tad.

"Go you," answered Ned promptly. "The one who loses has to get up and cook the breakfast."

CHAPTER IV

SURPRISED BY AN UNWELCOME VISITOR

"I'm sorry I was to blame for your going into the creek," apologized Ned Rector, bending over the shivering Stacy.

"I fell in, didn't I?" grinned the fat boy.

"No, you rolled in. My, but that water was cold!"

"B-r-r-r!" shivered Stacy, as the recollection of his icy bath came back to him. "Di - did you win the race?"

"Tad won it. I've got to get up and cook the breakfast, and it wasn't my turn at all. It was Tad's turn."

"Yab-hum," yawned Stacy, "I'm awful sleepy."

"So am I," answered Ned, uttering a long-drawn yawn.

"See here, Master Ned. Get out of those wet pajamas, rub yourself down thoroughly and put on a dry suit. I can't have you all sick on my hands to-morrow," commanded the Professor.

"Don't worry about us," laughed Ned. "It takes more than a bath in a cold creek to lay us up, eh, Tad?"

"I hope so," answered Tad Butler, who had rubbed himself until his body glowed. "But I thought once or twice that I was a goner while I was holding to that rock. I could not make Chunky try to support himself at all. He just clung to me until he fagged me all out."

"Come now, young gentlemen, down with this coffee and into the blankets."

Professor Zepplin had prepared the coffee, with which to warm the lads up, and had heated in the camp-fire some good sized boulders, which he wrapped in blankets and tucked in their beds. Chunky was the only one of the boys who did not protest. Ned and Tad objected to being "babied" as they called it, and when the Professor was not looking, they quickly rolled the feet warmers out at the foot of their beds.

Early next morning they were aroused by the cook's welcome call to breakfast. None of the lads seemed to be any the worse for his exciting experiences in the creek, much to the relief of Professor Zepplin, who feared the icy bath might at least bring on heavy colds.

Tumbling from their cots, they quickly washed; and then sprinting back and forth a few times, stirred up their circulation, after which the boys sat down to the morning meal with keen appetites.

Ned had cooked a liberal supply of bacon and potatoes and boiled a large pot of coffee.

Stacy opened his mouth as if he were about to yawn.

"Don't you dare to do that," warned Ned, waving the coffee pot threateningly. "The first boy who yawns to-day gets into trouble. And Stacy Brown, if you fall in the river again you'll get out the best way you can alone. We won't help you, remember that."

"This bacon looks funny," retorted Stacy, holding up a piece at the end of his fork. "Kind of looks as if something had happened to it."

"Just what I was going to say," added Walter.

"Yes, what has happened to it? It's as black as the Professor's hat."

All eyes were fixed upon the cook. "I don't care, I couldn't help it. If any of you fellows think you can do any better, you just try it. Cook your own meals if you don't like my way of serving them up. It wasn't my turn to get the breakfast, anyway."

"Our cook evidently has a grouch on this morning," laughed Walter. "Doesn't agree with him to take a midnight bath."

"The bath was all right, but I object to having my cooking criticised."

"The bacon does look peculiar," decided Professor Zepplin, sniffing gingerly at his own piece.

Ned's face flushed.

"What did you do to it to give it that peculiar shade, young man?"

"Why, I soused it in the creek to wash it off, then laid it in the fire to cook," replied Ned.

"In the fire?" shouted Tad.

"Of course. How do you expect I cooked it?" demanded the boy irritably. "I cooked it in the fire."

"I could do better'n that myself," muttered Stacy.

"Didn't you use the spider?" asked Walter.

"Spider? No. I didn't know you used a spider. Do you?"

"He cooked it in the fire," groaned Tad.

"Peculiar, very peculiar to say the least," decided the Professor grimly. "Gives it that peculiar sooty flavor, common to smoked ham I think we shall have to elect a new cook if you cannot do better than that. However, we'll manage to get along very well with this meal. If we have to get others we will hold a consultation as to the latest and most approved methods of doing so," he added, amid a general laugh at Ned's expense.

Breakfast over, blankets were rolled and packed on the ponies. About nine o'clock the Pony Riders set out for the foothills, after first having consulted their compasses and decided upon the course they were to follow to reach the point, some fifteen miles distant, where they expected to pick up the guide.

"Seems good to be in the saddle once more, doesn't it?" smiled Walter, after they had gotten well under way.

"Beats being in the river at midnight," laughed Tad. "Bad-eye looks as if he needed grooming, too. Ned, I take back all I said about the bacon this morning. You did me a good turn last night. If it hadn't been for you, Chunky and I wouldn't be here now. I couldn't have held to that rock much longer."

"Neither could I," interjected Stacy wisely.

Ned gave him a withering glance.

"You are an expert at falling in, but when it comes to getting out, that's another matter."

"How blue those mountains look!" marveled Walter, shading his eyes and gazing off toward the Rosebud Range.

"I hear there are some lawless characters in there, too," Tad answered thoughtfully.

"Where'd your hear that?" demanded Ned.

"Heard some men talking about it in the hotel back at Forsythe."

"Mustn't believe all you hear. What did they say?"

"Acting upon your advice, I should say that you wouldn't believe it if I told you," answered Tad sharply. "These men are a kind of outlaws, I believe. They steal horses and cattle. Probably sell the hides - I don't know. Somehow the Government officers have not been able to catch them, let alone to find out who they are."

"Indians, probably," replied Ned. "The country is full of them about here, so I hear."

"Mustn't believe all you hear," piped up Stacy, repeating Ned Rector's own words, and the latter's muttered reply was lost in the laughter that followed.

It was close to twelve o'clock when they finally emerged on a broad table or mesa. Before them lay the foothills of the Rosebud, rising in broken mounds, some of which towered almost level with the lower peaks of the mountains themselves.

"I don't see anything of our guide's cabin," said Tad, halting and looking about them. "What do you think, Professor!"

"We will go on to the foothills and wait there. I imagine he will he waiting for us somewhere hereabouts."

"Yes, we have followed our course by the compass," answered Tad.

However, the lad had overlooked the fact, as had the others, that in order to find a suitable fording place, they had followed the hanks of the East Fork for several miles. This served to throw them off their course and when they finally reached the foothills they were some six miles to the north of the place where the guide was to pick them up.

As they rode on, the ground gradually rose under them, nor did they realize that they were entering the foothills themselves; and so it continued until they finally found themselves surrounded by hills, narrow draws and broad, rocky gorges.

"Young gentlemen, I think we had better halt right

here. We shall be lost if we continue any farther," decided the Professor. "This is a nice level spot with just enough trees to give us shade. I propose that we dismount and make camp."

"Yes, we haven't had the tents up since we were in the Rockies," replied Ned. "We shall be forgetting how to pitch them soon if we do not have some practice."

On this trip, besides their small tents, the Pony Riders had brought with them canvas for a nine by twelve feet tent, which they proposed to use for a dining tent in wet weather, as well as a place for social gathering whenever the occasion demanded its use. They named it the parlor.

In high spirits, the lads leaped from their ponies and began removing their packs. Stacy Brown began industriously tugging at the fastenings which held the large tent to the back of the pack pony.

'I can't get it loose," he shouted. "What kind of hitch do you call this, anyway?"

"Young man, that's a squaw hitch. Ever hear of it before?" laughed Tad.

"No. What kind of hitch is a squaw hitch?" asked Chunky.

"Probably one that the braves use to tie up their wives with when they get lazy," Ned informed him.

"I know," spoke up Walter. "It's a hitch used to fasten the packs to the ponies. Mr. Stallings explained that to me when we were in Texas."

"Right," announced Tad, skillfully loosening the hitch, thus allowing the canvas of the parlor tent to fall to the ground.

While Tad and Walter were doing this, Professor Zepplin with Stacy had started off with hatchets to cut poles for the tents.

The sleeping tents were erected in a straight row with the parlor tent set up to the rear some few rods, backing up against the hills nearest to the mountains.

In front of the small tents the ponies were tethered out among the trees so as to be in plain view of the boys in case of trouble. Profiting from past experiences, they knew that without their mounts they would find themselves helpless.

In an hour the camp was pitched and the boys stood off to view the effect of their work.

"Looks like a military camp," said Ned.

"All but the guns," replied Walter. "We might stack our rifles outside here to make it look more military like."

"Let's do it." suggested Tad.

Laughing joyously, the lads got out their rifles, standing them on their stocks, with the muzzles together in front of the small tents. Not being equipped with bayonets the guns refused to stand alone, so they bound the muzzles together with twine wrapped about the sights. This held them firmly.

"There!" glowed Ned. "Where's the flag? Somebody get that and I'll cut a pole for it," suggested Tad Butler.

In a few moments Old Glory was waving idly in the gentle summer breeze and the boys, doffing their hats, gave three cheers and a tiger for it, in which Professor Zepplin joined with almost boyish enthusiasm.

"I always take off my hat to that beautiful flag," said the Professor, gazing up at it admiringly.

"How about your own country's flag?" teased Ned.

"That is it. I am an American citizen. Your flag is my flag. And now that we have done homage to our country and our flag, supposing we consult our own bodily comfort by getting dinner. Of course, if you young gentlemen are not hungry we can skip the noon -- "

"Not hungry? Did you ever hear of our skipping a meal when we could get it?" protested Walter.

"For a young man with a delicate appetite, you do very well," laughed the Professor. "It wag less than two months ago, if I remember correctly, that the doctors thought you were not going to live, you were so delicate."

"Almost as delicate as Chunky now," chuckled Ned maliciously.

The midday meal was more successful than had been their breakfast. They ate it under the trees, deciding to dine in the parlor tent just at dusk.

Frank Gee Patchin

The afternoon was spent in shooting, at which the boys were becoming quite proficient. By this time, even Stacy Brown could be trusted to manage his own rifle without endangering the lives of his companions.

"Is there any game in these hills?" asked Ned, while he was refilling the magazine of his repeating rifle.

"Plenty of it, I am told," replied the Professor. "There is big game all over the state."

"What kind?"

"Bears, mountain lions and the like."

"W-h-e-w. That sounds interesting. May we go gunning to-morrow?"

"Better wait until the guide joins us. It will be best to have some one with us who understands the habits of the animals. As you have learned, hunting big game is not boys' play," concluded the Professor.

"Yes, I remember our experience in hunting the cougar in the Rockies. I guess I'll wait."

During the afternoon, the boys made short trips along the foothills hoping to find some trace of the guide, but search as they would they were unable to locate him. Nor did they dare stray far from the camp for fear of being unable to find their way back. The foothills all looked so alike that if one unfamiliar with them should lose his way he would find himself in a serious predicament.

"I guess we shall have to camp here for the rest of the

summer," Professor Zepplin said, while they were eating their supper. "We must be a long distance from our man if he has not heard our shooting this afternoon."

The boys were enjoying themselves, however; in addition, there was a sense of independence that they had not felt before. They were alone and entirely on their own resources, which of itself added to the zest of the trip.

The supper dishes having been cleared away and the camp-fire stirred up to a bright, cheerful blaze, all hands gathered in the parlor tent for an evening chat.

Above them swung an oil lantern which dimly shed its rays over the little company. Professor Zepplin was poring over an old volume that he had brought with him, while the boys were discussing the merits of their new ponies, which by this time had developed their individual peculiarities.

Chunky, growing sleepy, had crawled to the rear of the tent, where he sat leaning against the closed flap, nodding drowsily.

Finally they saw him straighten up and brush a hand over the back of his head.

"He's dreaming," laughed Ned. "Imagines he's rolling down the river bank again."

Suddenly they were aroused by the fat boy's voice raised in angry protest.

"Stop tickling my neck," he growled, vigorously

rubbing that part of his anatomy. "Funny, you fellows can't let me alone."

"You must be having bad dreams," laughed Ned. "We are not bothering you. We're all over here."

"Yes, you are. You've done it three times and you woke me up," answered the fat boy, settling back and closing his eyes preparatory to renewing his disturbed nap.

He was asleep in a moment, not having heeded the laughter of his companions, nor their noisy comments.

But Stacy dozed for a moment only. He sat up quickly and very straight, while a shrewd expression appeared in his eyes. Had they been looking they might have observed one of his hands being drawn cautiously behind him, as if he were reaching for something. The boys were too busy, however, to pay any heed to the lad, and the Professor was deeply absorbed in his book.

"I've got you this time! Tell me you weren't tickling my neck? I'll show you Stacy Brown's not the sleepy head you -- "

The boy paused suddenly and scrambling to all fours turned about on his hands and knees, intently gazing at the flap against which he had been leaning.

"What's the matter, gone crazy over there!" called Tad. "Anybody would think you had from the racket you are making."

Stacy did not answer. He had not even heard Tad speak to him. His eyes, bulging with fear, were fixed on the flap. What he saw was a long black snout poked through the slit in the canvas, and just back of that a pair of beady, evil eyes.

"Y-e-o-w!" yelled Stacy. The lad leaped to his feet and dashed from the tent, bowling over Walter and Tad as he ran, shouting in his fright and crying for help. Knowing instinctively that something really serious had happened, the others sprang up, peering at the other end of the tent. For a moment, they could see nothing in the flickering shadows; then as their eyes became more accustomed to the half light, they discovered what filled them with alarm as well.

"Run for your lives!" shouted Tad, bolting from the tent in a single leap, followed almost instantly by Ned Rector and Walter Perkins.

The Professor with one startled glance, hurled his precious book at the object he saw entering the tent at the back, and bolted through the front opening, taking the end tent pole down with him in his hasty flight.

CHAPTER V

THE PURSUIT OF THE BURNING BEAR

What is it?" cried Walter breathlessly, slowing up when he observed that the others were doing likewise. "It's a bear, I think," replied the Professor. "I only saw the head so I can't be sure. Keep away. Where is Stacy?"

"I - I think he's running, still," answered Ned, his voice somewhat shaky.

"There goes the other tent pole down!" shouted Tad.

"He's wrecking the place. That's too bad," groaned Walter.

"Are the provisions all in there?" asked the Professor anxiously.

"No, most of them are over in my tent, where I took them from the pack pony," Ned informed him.

"We are that much ahead anyway. I think we had better get a little further away, young gentlemen. We had better get near trees so we can make a fairly dignified escape if that fellow concludes to come out after us."

"He's too busy just now," announced Tad, with an attempt at laughter.

"Get the guns," ordered the Professor.

"I can't," cried Tad.

"Why can't you? I will get them myself."

"They are all in that tent there with the bear," groaned Tad.

"There's a box of shells in there, too," added Walter. "I put it there myself."

"Then, indeed, we had better take to the trees," decided Professor Zepplin.

"Wait," warned Tad. "He won't get out right away. See, he has pulled the tent down about him."

"Yes, he's having the time of his life," nodded Ned. "I hope he never gets out. If we had our guns now!"

And, indeed, Mr. Bruin was having his own troubles. Angry snarls and growls could be heard under the heaving canvas as the black bear plunged helplessly about, twisting the tent about him in his desperate struggles to free himself.

They could hear the clatter of the tinware as he threshed about, and the crash and bang of other articles belonging to their equipment.

"Look! What's that light?" exclaimed Walter.

"Fire!" cried the Professor.

"The tent's on fire!" shouted Tad.

"Quick, get water!" urged Ned.

"What for? To put out the bear?" laughed Tad.

"I had forgotten about the lantern. That's what has caused the fire. When the tent collapsed the lantern went down with it, and in his floundering about he has managed to set the place on fire," the Professor informed them.

"There goes the parlor tent. That settles it," said Walter.

The other two boys groaned.

"Has he-ha-ha-has he gone?" wailed Chunky, peering from behind a tree.

"No, he hasn't gone. He's very much here. Don't you see that tent! What do you suppose is making it hump up in the middle, if he isn't there? And the tent's on fire, too," answered Ned, in a tone of disgust. "This is a bad start for sure."

"I didn't fall in that time, did I? I fell out," interrupted Stacy. "Lucky for me that I did, too. I would have been in a nice fix if that tent had come down on me and that animal at the same time." He shivered at the thought. "What is it, a lion?"

"Lion! No, you ninny, it's a bear. B-e-a-r," spelled Ned, with strong emphasis. "Do you understand that?"

"Y-y-e-s. I-I-I thought it was a lion. I did, honest," he muttered. "And it tickled my neck with its paw, too. Wow!"

Stacy instinctively moved further away from the tent.

Disturbing as their situation was at that moment. the lads could not repress a shout of laughter over Stacy's funny words. But Stacy's face was solemn. He saw nothing to laugh at.

"Lucky for both of you that you didn't yawn. The bear might nave fallen in," jeered Ned.

"Might have been a good thing for us if Chunky had yawned. Maybe the bear would have got to yawning at the same time, and yawned and yawned until he was so helpless that we could have captured him," laughed Walter.

"Not much chance of that," answered Tad. "Bears don't yawn until after a full meal. I guess our bear over there hasn't had one lately or he wouldn't have been nosing about our camp when we were all there."

"Keep back there, boys. Please don't get too close. He is liable to break out at any time. He is a small bear, but there is no telling what he may do in his rage when he emerges," warned the Professor.

"We're not afraid," answered Ned.

The boys, having no weapons, had armed themselves with clubs, prepared to do battle with their visitor should he chance to come their way.

"What's that racket over there in the bushes?" demanded Ned, wheeling sharply.

"It's the ponies," answered Tad, darting away.

At last the little animals had discovered the presence of the bear in camp and were making frantic efforts to break their tethers.

"Come over here, some of you. The bronchos are having a fit. I can't manage all of them at once," called Tad in an excited tone.

"What's the matter - are they afraid?" called the Professor.

"I should say they are. They'll get away from me if you don't hurry."

Leaving the hear to his own desperate efforts, the boys rushed to the aid of Tad Butler. They were not quick enough, however.

"There goes one of them!" cried Tad.

A pony had broken the rope and with a snort, had bounded away. Tad, leaped on the bare back of his own pony, first having caught up his lariat, and set out after the fleeing animal.

Luckily the runaway broncho had headed for the open and Tad was able to overhaul him before they had gone far from the camp.

Riding up beside the little animal it was an easy matter to drop the loop over his head and bring him down.

"There, that will teach you to run away," growled the boy, cinching the rope and dragging the unruly pony back to camp.

In the meantime the others, after considerable effort, had succeeded in securing the other plunging bronchos, more rope having been brought for the purpose, while Tad, breathing hard, staked down the frightened animal he had roped.

"Now we'll see how Mr. Bear is getting along," announced the Professor, as they turned back toward the camp, where the bear was still fighting desperately with the smouldering tent.

As they reached the scene they observed Professor Zepplin hurrying to his tent. He was back again almost at once.

"Just happened to think of my revolver," he explained.

"Think you can kill him with that?" asked Tad.

"I don't know. I can try. It's a thirty-eight calibre."

"Won't even feel it," sniffed Ned. "I've read lots of times that it takes a lot to kill a bear."

The Professor raised his weapon and fired at the spot where the tent appeared to be most active.

Though he had pulled the trigger only once a series of sudden explosions followed, seemingly coming from beneath the tent itself.

"What's that!" demanded the Professor, lowering his

own weapon, plainly puzzled.

"Guess the bear's shooting at us," suggested Chunky wisely.

"No. I know what it is," cried Tad.

"You know?" demanded Ned.

"Sure. It's our cartridges exploding. The fire from the lantern has got at those pasteboard boxes in which we carried the shells."

Now they were popping with great rapidity, and instinctively the boys drew further away from the danger zone, though the Professor told them the bullets could not hurt them, there being not sufficient force behind to carry them that distance.

The Professor stood his ground as an object lesson and again resumed his target practice. The tough canvas resisted the bear's efforts, and the fire was burning slowly. However, the tent seemed to be ruined and the boys feared their rifles would share a similar fate.

"He's breaking out!" yelled Chunky, who was some distance to the right of the others, now dancing up and down in his excitement. "Look out for him!"

With a last desperate effort, the animal had succeeded in forcing his way through the stubborn canvas.

"Look, look!" yelled Walter Perkins, greatly excited.

The spectacle was one that for the moment held the boys spellbound. A mass of flame separated itself from the ruins of the tent. With snarls of pain and rage the mass ambled rapidly away in a trail of fire.

"The bear's on fire!" shouted Ned Rector.

"Help!" screamed Chunky.

Blinded by the pain and the flames that had gotten into its eyes, the animal not seeing the lad, lurched heavily against him and Stacy Brown went down with a howl of terror.

The boy, who had not been harmed, was up like a flash, running from the fearful thing as fast as his short legs would carry him.

"Oh, that's too bad!" exclaimed Tad.

He did not refer to the accident to his companion, which he considered as too trivial to notice, but rather to the sufferings of the animal. Tad felt a deep sympathy for any dumb animal that was in trouble, no matter if it were a bear which would have shown him no mercy had they met face to face.

"Professor, let me have your revolver please," he cried.

"What for?"

"I want to put the brute out of his misery. Please do!"

"There are no more shells in it."

"Then load it. I'm going to get Pink-eye. Hurry, hurry! Can't you see how the miserable creature is suffering?"

The lad darted away for his pony, while Professor Zepplin, sharing something of the boy's own feelings, hurried to his tent and recharged his weapon.

He had no more than returned when Tad came dashing up on Pink-eye.

"Where is he? Do you see him?"

"Over there, I can see the fire in the bushes," answered Ned Rector.

"Quick, give me the gun," demanded Tad.

"Wait, I'll go with you," said Ned.

"No, remain where you are," ordered Professor Zepplin. "Some of you will surely be shot. Thaddeus, remember, you are not to go far from camp.

Tad was off in a twinkle. Putting the spurs to Pink-eye, the animal leaped from the camp and disappeared among the trees.

"I am afraid I should not have allowed him to go," announced the Professor, with a doubtful shake of his head. But it was too late now for regrets.

Tad found the going rough. He soon made out the flaming animal just ahead of him. The beast was down rolling from side to side in a frantic effort to put out the fire that was burning into his flesh.

Tad could not understand why the fur should make so much flame. He spurred the pony as near to the animal as he could get. Then he saw that the bear had become entangled in the guy ropes, and that he was pulling along with him portions of the burning canvas, attached to the ropes. It was this which made the animal a living torch.

The pony in its fright was rearing and plunging, bucking and squealing so that the lad had difficulty in keeping his seat.

"Steady, steady, Pink-eye," he soothed.

For an instant the broncho ceased its wild antics and stood trembling with fear.

"Bang!"

Tad had aimed the heavy revolver and pulled the trigger.

Instantly the pony went up into the air again and the lad gripped its sides with his legs, giving a gentle pressure with the spurs.

"Whoa, Pink-eye! I hit Mm, I did. I aimed for his head, but I must have merely grazed it. I wish I could kill the brute and put him out of his misery," said the lad more concerned for the suffering animal before him than for his own safety.

No sooner had he fired the first shot, than the bear sprang to its feet and sped away up a steep bank. Tad noticed that the bear's rolling had extinguished some of the fire, but he knew that it was still burrowing in the beast's fur, causing him great agony.

"I am too far away to hit him. I've got to get closer,"

decided the boy. "Pink-eye, do you think you can make that climb?"

The pony shook its head and rattled the bits in its mouth.

"All right, old chap, try it."

A cluck and a gentle slap on the broncho's flanks sent him straight for the steep bank. At first his feet slipped under him; he stumbled, righted himself and digging in the slender hoofs fairly lifted himself up and up. In the meantime Mr. Bruin was making better progress. He seemed unable to escape from the fire, but he could get away from this new enemy, the gun in the hands of the boy on the horse.

Every little while as he found he had gained on his pursuer the bear would throw himself down, and with snarls and angry growls, take a few awkward rolls; then be up and off again.

Once more the lad thought he was near enough to take another shot.

Releasing the reins and dropping them to the pony's neck, he steadied the hand that held the gun with the left and fired.

"Oh, pshaw, I missed him!" he groaned. "That's too bad. I'm only adding to his misery. Next time I'll get nearer to him before I try to shoot."

He went at Pink-eye, applying every method with which he was familiar to increase the pony's speed. Pink-eye responded as best he could, and began climbing the hill that had now developed into a fair sized mountain, making even more rapid headway than the bear himself.

"Good boy," encouraged Tad. "We'll overhaul him if you can keep that up. Steady now. Don't slip or you'll tumble me down the hill and yourself, too. Steady, Pink-eye. W-h-o-e-e!"

"Bang!"

The bear was running broadside to him and the lad could not resist taking another shot at it. Like the previous effort, however, he had failed.

Tad tittered an exclamation of disgust and put spurs to the pony.

"I never did know how to handle a revolver," he complained. "I'll begin to practise with this gun to-morrow if I get out of this scrape safely."

He had failed to take into consideration that a bear was an extremely difficult animal to kill, and that frequently one of them could carry many bullets in its body without seeming to be bothered at all.

But the lad was determined to get this one. He had not thought of where he was going nor how far from camp he had strayed. His one desire now was to get the animal and put a quick end to it.

This time Tad was enabled to get closer to Bruin than at any time during the chase. He drove the pony at a gallop right up alongside of the animal.

Leaning over he aimed the gun at the beast's head, holding it firmly with both hands.

Tad gave the trigger a quick, firm pressure. A sharp explosion followed.

At the same instant, Pink-eye in a frightened effort to get clear of the bear, leaped to one side. The lad, leaning over from the saddle, was taken unawares, and making a desperate effort to grasp the saddle pommel, Tad was hurled sideways to the ground.

"Whoa, Pink-eye!" he commanded sharply as he was falling. But Pink-eye refused to obey. The pony uttered a loud snort and plunged into the bushes. There he paused, wheeled, and peered out suspiciously at the boy and the bear.

Tad's shot had gone home. His aim had been true. Yet the sting of the bullet served only to anger the bear still further. With an angry growl, it turned and charged the lad ferociously.

In falling, the plucky boy had struck on his head and shoulders, the fall partially stunning him. For an instant, he pivoted on his head, then toppling over on his back, he lay still.

Powerless to move a muscle, the lad was dimly conscious of a hulking figure standing over him, its hot breath on his face. His right hand clutched the revolver, but he seemed unable to raise it.

A loud explosion sounded in Tad Butler's ears, then sudden darkness overwhelmed him.

CHAPTER VI

LOST IN THE ROSEBUD RANGE

"Whoa, Pink-eye!" muttered the lad, stirring restlessly. "I'll get him next time. Look out, he's charging us. Oh!"

The boy suddenly opened his eyes. The darkness about him was deep and impenetrable and he was conscious of a heavy weight on his chest. What it was, he did not know, and some moments passed before he had recovered sufficiently to form an intelligent idea of what had happened.

All at once he recollected.

"It was the bear," he murmured. "I wonder if I am dead!"

No, he could feel the ground under him, and a rock that his right hand rested on, felt cold and chilling. But what of the pressure on his chest?

Cautiously the lad moved a hand toward the object that was holding him down. His fingers lightly touched it.

Tad could scarce repress a yell.

It was the head of the bear that was resting on him, and he had no idea whether the animal were dead or asleep, awaiting the moment when the lad should stir again to fasten its cruel teeth into his body.

The boy was satisfied, however, that by exerting all his strength he would be able to pull himself away before the beast could awaken, even, providing it were still alive.

First he sought cautiously for his weapon, his fingers groping about over the ground at his right hand. He could not find it. Undoubtedly it had fallen underneath the bear.

Tad determined to mate a desperate effort to escape. He felt as if his hair were standing on end.

With a cry that he could not keep back, the lad whirled over and sprang to his feet. As he did so he leaped away, running with all his might until he had put some distance between himself and the prostrate animal.

Realizing that he was not being followed, Tad brought up sharply and dodged behind a tree. There he stood listening intently for several minutes.

Not a sound disturbed the stillness of the night. The leaves of the trees hung limp and lifeless, for no breeze was stirring.

"I wonder if he's dead," whispered the lad, almost afraid to trust his voice out loud. "Maybe that shot finished him. I must find out somehow."

Tad searched his clothes for matches, finally finding

his match safe. Next he sought to gather some sticks with which to make a torch, but the only wood he was able to find was of oak and so green that it would not burn.

"That's too bad," he muttered. "I'll have to try it with the matches."

Lighting one he picked his way carefully toward the place where he had been lying, peering into the shadows ahead of him suspiciously as he went.

"There he is," breathed Tad.

He could faintly make out the figure of the bear lying half on its side as it had been before, the only difference being that the animal's head was stretched out on the ground instead of on the lad's chest.

"I believe he's dead. He must be or he'd have been after me before this," decided the boy. "I 'm going to find out."

Mustering his courage, Tad continued his cautious approach, lighting match after match, shading the flame with his hands so that the light would not get into his eyes and prevent him from seeing anything ahead of him.

It required no little courage for a boy alone in the mountains to walk up to a bear, not knowing whether the animal were dead or alive. Yet when Tad Butler made up his mind to do a certain thing, he persisted until he had accomplished it.

He reached the side of the animal, that is, close enough

so that he could get a good view of it.

The bear never moved and Tad drew closer, walking on his toes that he might make no sound. There seemed no other way to make certain except to stir the animal.

"I'll do it," whispered Tad.

Cautiously lighting another match he drew back his left foot and administered a sound kick to the beast's side.

Thinking that the bear had moved under the blow, Tad whirled and ran tittering a loud "Oh!"

He waited, but could hear no sound.

"I believe I am afraid of myself. That bear hasn't stirred at all. I'm going back this time and make sure."

He did. But this time, steeling himself to the task, Tad stood still after he had prodded the beast with his foot again. There was no movement other than a slight tremor caused by the impact of the kick.

"Hurrah, I've shot a bear!" cried the lad in the excess of his excitement. "I wonder what the boys will say. The next question is how am I going to get him back to camp?"

Tad pondered over this problem some moments.

"I know," he cried. "I'll hitch a rope to him and make Pink-eye tow him out. But where is that pony?"

All at once the realization came to him that the pony

had thrown him off. That was the last he had seen of Pink-eye.

Tad whistled and called, listening after each attempt without the slightest result.

"He's gone. I've got to find my way back as best I can. The worst of it is I may be a long way from camp, but I guess I can find my way with the compass all right."

The compass, however, was nowhere to be found. The lad went through his pockets twice in search of it.

"Pshaw! Just my luck. I'm as bad at losing things as Chunky is in falling in. I'll get the gun anyway, for the Professor will be provoked if I go back without it. Ah, there it is."

Tad picked up the weapon joyfully.

"I've got something to defend myself with, at least," he told himself. A moment later when he discovered that the weapon held nothing but empty shells, the keen edge of his joy was dulled.

"Well, it's better to pack back an empty gun than no gun at all," he decided philosophically. Let me see, I think we came up that way. They'll build a big fire so I can see it and I ought to be there within half an hour at least."

The lad struck out confidently. He had been lost in the wilderness before, and though he felt a slight uneasiness he had no doubt of his ability to find the camp eventually.

He walked vigorously for half an hour. Then he halted. The same impressive silence surrounded him.

"I think I have been going a little too far to the left," he decided. He changed his course and plodded on methodically again.

Another half hour passed and once more the lad paused, this time with the realization strong upon him that he had lost his way.

Placing both hands to his mouth Tad uttered a long drawn "C-o-o-e-e-e!" He listened intently, then repeated the call.

The sound of his own voice almost frightened him.

"Oh, I'm lost!" he cried, now fully appreciating his position.

The panic of the lost seized him and Tad ran this way and that, plunging ahead for some distance, then swerving to the right or to the left in a desperate attempt to free himself from the endless thicket, bruising his body from contact with the trunks of the trees and cutting his hands as they struck the rocks violently when he fell.

"Tad Butler, you stop this!" he commanded sternly, bringing himself up sharply. "I didn't think you were such a silly kid as to be afraid of the dark." But in his innermost heart the lad knew that it was not the shadows that had so upset him. It was the feeling of being lost in an unknown forest.

Instead of being in the foothills as he had supposed, he was penetrating the fastnesses of the Rosebud

Mountains themselves.

"There is no use in my going on like this," he decided finally. "I'll sit down and wait for daylight. That's all I can do. I surely can find my way back to camp when the l ight comesagain."

The next question was where should he go - where find a safe place to stay until morning. Tad remembered with a start that there were bears in the range. He knew this from his own recent experience. How many other savage beasts there might be in the woods he did not know. He had heard some one speak of mountain lions, and having seen these before, he fervently hoped he might not have another experience with them, unarmed as he was.

"If this gun only were loaded, I should feel better."

After searching around for some time, Tad found a ledge that seemed to rise to a considerable height. Up this he clambered. It would give him a good view in the morning anyway, besides protecting him from any prowling animals that might chance in that part of the forest.

Tad ensconced himself in a slight depression, and with a flat rock for a resting place, leaned back determined to make the best of his position.

A gentle breeze now stirred the foliage above his head and all about him until the sound became a restless murmur, as if Nature were holding council over the lad's predicament.

The lost boy did not so interpret the sounds, however.

He made a more practical application of them.

"It's going to rain," he decided wisely, casting a glance above him at the sky, which was becoming rapidly overcast. "And I haven't any umbrella," he added, grinning at his own feeble joke. "Well, I've been wet before. I cannot well be any more so than I was last night. I'll bet the rainwater will be warmer than the waters in the East Fork. If it isn't I'll surely freeze to death."

Fortunately he bad worn his coat when he left the camp, else he would now have suffered from the cold. As it was, he shivered, but more from nervousness than from the chill night air.

"Yoh - hum, but I'm sleepy," he murmured drowsily. A moment more and his head had drooped to one side and Tad Butler was sleeping as soundly as if tucked away between his own blankets back in his tent in the foothills.

CHAPTER VII

ALMOST BETRAYED BY A SNEEZE

Tad awakened with a start.

His first impression was that he smelled smoke, and for the moment he believed himself back in camp. A movement convinced him of his error. A jagged point of rock had cut into his flesh while he slept. He almost cried out with the pain of it, and as he moved a little to shift his body from it, the wound hurt worse than ever.

The lad was still surrounded by an impenetrable darkness. It all came back to him - but standing out stronger than all the rest was the fact that he was lost.

"Wonder how long I've slept," he muttered. "Seems as if I had been here a year. Lucky I awoke or I'd been stuck fast on that rock, for good and all. Whew! B-r-r-r! I think it's going to snow. Thought it was going to rain just before I went to sleep. Wonder if they have snow up here in the summer time. Have almost everything else," continued the lad, muttering to himself, half under his breath.

Slowly rising he shook himself vigorously and rubbed his palms together to get his circulation stirred up.

Frank Gee Patchin

"Hello, what's that? I remember now, I smelled smoke or thought I did."

Tad sniffed the chill air suspiciously.

"It is smoke," he decided. "Maybe I've set the woods on fire with my matches. Guess I'll climb down and investigate."

He started to move down the side of the ledge when it occurred to him that perhaps it would be better to investigate from where he was; he did not know what danger he might be running into if he were to climb down without first having made sure that it was perfectly safe to do so. Just what he might meet with he did not know. But he felt an uneasy sense of impending danger.

"Often feel that way when I first wake up, especially if I've been eating pie the night before," he confided to himself, in order to urge his courage back to life.

Bending forward he peered from side to side, but was unable to find a single trace of light, anywhere about him. If it were a fire it must be some distance away, he concluded.

"If it were some distance away, I wouldn't smell it. The wind has died down. No, the fire that smoke comes from is right near by me," he whispered.

The sense of human habitation near him caused his pulses to beat more rapidly. The question that remained for him to decide, was who was it that had started the fire?

Tad Butler determined to find out if possible, and at once.

He crept cautiously to the right, feeling his way along the ledge, not being sure how near he was to the edge. He found it more suddenly than he had expected, and narrowly missed falling over head first.

"Whew! That was a close call," he muttered. "I must be more careful."

There was no sign of either smoke or fire below him, as he observed after getting his balance again. He drew back cautiously and worked his way to the side that he had been facing, yet with no better result than before.

There yet remained two sides to be investigated - the one he had climbed up and the other that lay to the left of him. Tad chose the latter as the most likely to give him the information he sought. However, he found that the edge lay some distance away. The table of rock was much wider than he had imagined, when he first ascended to it.

The way was rough. Once the lad's foot slipped into a crevice. In seeking to withdraw it he gave the ankle a wrench that caused him to settle down on the rocks with a half moan of pain. His shoe had become wedged in between the rocks so that he had difficulty in withdrawing it at all, and the injured ankle gave him a great deal of pain as he struggled to release himself.

"Guess I'll have to take off my shoe. Hope I haven't sprained my ankle. I'll be in a fine mess if I have," he grumbled.

The ankle gave him considerable trouble; but he rubbed it all of ten minutes, and he found that he could endure his shoe again. He was full of curiosity as well as anxiety to learn the cause of the smoke, which, by this time, seemed to be coming his way in greater volume.

After having relaced the shoe and leggin, Tad started on again, this time on all fours, not trusting himself to try to walk, feeling his way ahead of him with his hands, which he considered the safer way to do.

"There's somebody down there," he whispered, after a long interval of slow creeping over the rocks. "I wonder who it is? Perhaps they are looking for me. I'll give them a surprise if they are."

The surprise, however, was to be Tad's.

At last he reached the edge of the little butte. Slowly stretching his neck and lying flat on his stomach, he peered over.

A cloud of black smoke rolled up into his face, causing the lad to withdraw hastily.

"Aka-c-h-e-w," sneezed Tad, burying his face in his hands.

"Whew, what a smudge! I'll bet they heard that sneeze."

"What's that?" demanded a gruff voice below. "Sounded like somebody sneezing."

"No, it's an owl," replied another. "I've heard that kind

before. Sometimes you'd think it was a fellow snoring."

"Must be funny kind of a bird," grunted the first speaker.

"He's right. That's exactly what I am," growled Tad, who had plainly overheard their conversation. Yet he was thankful that the men below had not realized the truth. Tad was quite willing to be mistaken for a bird under the circumstances.

After making sure that the men were not going to investigate the sound, the boy crept again toward the edge, working to the right a little further this time, so that the smoke might not smite him full in the face as had been the case before.

There were four of them - strangers. The boy observed that they were dressed like cowboys, broad brimmed hats, blue shirts and all. From the belt of each was suspended a holster from which protruded the butt of a heavy revolver.

"Cowboys," he breathed. "At least they ought to be and I hope they are nothing else."

The lad's attention was fixed particularly on one of the party. He was all of six feet tall, powerfully built, his swarthy face covered with a scraggly growth of red beard, and with a face of a peculiarly sinister appearance.

"When do they expect the herd?" asked the first speaker.

"Be here the day after tomorrer I reckon," answered the man with the red beard.

"How many?"

"They say there's five thousand sheep in the herd, but it's more'n likely there'll be ten when they git here."

"Huh!" grunted the other.

"There'll be less when we git through with them."

"You bet."

"Boss Simms will be mad. He'll be ripping, when we clean him out."

Two of the men rose at the big fellow's direction and stalked off into the bushes to attend to their ponies, which the lad could hear stirring restlessly, but could not see.

"Simms!" breathed Tad. "What does this mean? Those men are up to some mischief. I know it. I must find out what it is they are planning to do."

Tad learned a few moments later, but in his attempts to overhear what the plans of these strange men were, he nearly lost his own life.

CHAPTER VIII

INTO THE ENEMY'S CAMP

"Has Simms been warned that he'd better keep them out of this here territory?" asked one.

"Yes."

"Who told him?"

"Bob Moore, who owns the Double X Ranch on the west side of the range. I saw to that," announced the man with the beard.

Tad decided that he was the leader of the party, but it was not yet clear what they were planning to do. Yet he knew that if he listened long enough something was sure to be dropped that would give him a clue to the mystery.

"Bob's mad as a trapped bear over it. Swears he'll kill every sheep in the country before he'll let Simms drive in the new herd and graze it here."

"Suppose you put it into his head proper like to do something?" laughed one.

"Well, I did talk it over with him a bit," admitted the

leader. "But he wasn't hard to show."

"When is the thing coming off?"

"We haven't decided yet. We four will talk that over. Perhaps the same night they get in. They'll be restless then and easy to start."

"But won't the foreman corral the sheep?"

"Don't think so. Haven't room. They haven't fixed up a new corral, because they expected to graze the sheep on north. That many will clean up the range right straight ahead of us for more'n a hundred miles, so that we cattle men won't have half a chance to graze our cattle," grinned the spokesman of the party.

His companions laughed harshly.

"I reckon," answered another. "We'll have all the cattle men on both sides of the Rosebud range so stirred up that they will pitch into that flock like hyenas who haven't had a square meal since snow fell last. When they break loose there's going to be fun, now I tell you. That's the time we get busy. We ought to be able to get a thousand of them anyhow. Before next morning we'll be so far down toward the Big Horn range that they won't catch us. And besides, after the cattle men get through killing mutton, a thousand more or less won't be missed. It'll make a nice bunch to add to our flock. If we work that a few times we'll have enough to make a shipment worth while."

"So that's the game is it?" muttered Tad Butler. "Well, they won't do it if I can help it." Yet be realized how powerless he was at that moment to defeat their nefarious plans.

Somehow they were going to urge the real cattle men to use highhanded measures to destroy Mr. Simms's flock. They were going to scatter them, and then these men were going to make off with all they could drive away. It did not seem to the listening boy that such things were possible; yet Mr. Simms was authority for the statement that such acts were not unknown in this far northern state.

There were still many points that Tad was not clear on, but he had heard enough to enable him to give the rancher a timely warning of what they proposed to do.

The lad knew what that meant. It meant trouble. His sympathies had been largely with the cattle men - he had looked down on the sheep industry and for the reason that he knew only what the cattle men had told him about it.

At that moment Tad Butler was experiencing a change of heart. That they could plan ruthlessly to slaughter the inoffensive little animals passed his comprehension. A remark below him caused the lad to prick up his ears and listen intently.

"As I came over the Little Muddy this afternoon, I thought I saw some sort of a camp in the foothills," said a voice. "Thought mebby that might be the outfit, though I couldn't see what they were doing on that side of the range."

"Oh," laughed the big man, "I know the one you mean. Yes, I took a look at that outfit myself."

"Oh, he did, eh? Wonder we didn't see him," grunted Tad, realizing that the men referred to the camp of the Pony Riders. "There was something besides bears around there, I see."

"Find out what it was!"

"Yes, it seemed to be a camp of boys. There was only one man in the bunch so far as I could see. He was a tall gent with whiskers that hadn't been shaved for two weeks o' Sundays."

Tad could not repress a laugh.

"I wish the boys could hear that," he said, laughing softly. "That hits off the Professor better than a real picture could do."

"Huh! What were they doing!"

"You can search me for the answer. I haven't got it," laughed the big fellow. "We don't need to bother about them. They're out here with some crazy idea in their tops. They can't interfere with our plans any."

"You'd better not be too sure about that," chuckled Tad. "Perhaps one of them may if he has the good luck to get out of here without being discovered."

"What's the plan, Bluff?"

"So that's his name? I'll remember that," muttered Tad.

"That's what I wanted you boys to meet me here for. I want you to see all the ranchers before to-morrow night on both sides of the Rosebud. Understand now, no blunt giving away of the game. You want to start by telling them you hear Boss Simms is bringing in ten thousand head of sheep, and that he's going to graze them up the valley all the way over the free grass to the north. Tell them that it'll be mighty poor picking for the cows and so on until you get 'em good and properly mad -- "

"Yes, what then?"

"Better let the ranchers make threats first, then you can say that you hear the others are going to teach Boss Simms a lesson and stampede his flock to-morrow or next night. Say you hear the word will go out when the mine is ready to touch a match to. You'll know how to work it?"

"Sure thing, Bluff. Who do you want us to see?"

"I want you and Jake to take the west side of the mountains. Lazy and I will take the east. Work it thoroughly and don't you go to making any bad breaks. Right after the job is over, besides the sheep we get for our own herd, there'll be a few thousand laying dead around these parts. We'll take the contract to skin them for the hides. That'll be another rake off. Do you follow me?"

"Yes."

"To-morrow night meet me at the Three Sisters and I'll be able to give you your orders for the rest of the boys."

"You don't think they'll suspect you - that they'll be wise to what the game is?" asked one of the men apprehensively.

"No fear of that. They'd never mix me up with any such deal as that. I'm a respectable law abiding rancher, I am," laughed the man with the red beard. "Don't you go to getting cold feet. That's the sure way to get caught," admonished the leader.

"Want us to start now?"

"No, sure not. What's the use? We'd better turn in and get some sleep. It'll be light enough by three o'clock in the morning. We'll get a rasher of bacon and some hot coffee, then we'll light out for the valley. You know you don't have to see Bob Moore. And better not go near the Circle T Ranch. I'm not any too sure about those fellows. We'll turn in now."

"I've heard enough to hang the whole bunch," thought Tad Butler. "The trouble is I don't know who they are. But that does not make so much difference. Only if I did know, Mr. Simms might be able to have them arrested. As it is, I guess the best he can do is to get ready to fight them off when they do come," reasoned the lad.

"Better stake the ponies nearer camp in case anything comes along. I came across bear tracks a few miles to the east of here," the big man advised them."

"So did I," thought Tad.

"I forgot to tell you that there'll be three or four Crow braves with us on the raid as well as half a dozen Blackfeet?"

"Blackfeet? What are them redskins doing down here, off the reservation?" demanded Jake.

"They're like all critters, think the pasture over the fence is better'n their own," laughed Bluff. "Guess there's no need of any of us keeping awake. We ain't likely to have any surprises."

The cowboy outlaw, however, was about to have the most surprising of surprises that could have come to him at that time.

Tad, in his anxiety to catch every word that was uttered, had drawn his body close up to the edge of the cliff, his head and shoulders hanging well over.

In front of him, right down to the camp stretched a long, sloping rock, whose smooth face, glistened in the light of the camp fire. As the men rose to prepare for the night, Tad began pulling himself cautiously back, bracing himself with one hand.

Suddenly the hand slipped. How it happened he was unable to tell afterward, but instantly Tad was over the rock and tobogganing down its side head first.

A spot rougher than the rest of the rock, caught in his clothes, righting the boy's body, permitting him to shoot down the rest of the way, feet first.

The Pony Rider Boy's presence of mind did not desert him for an instant. It was not a long drop. He felt that he would land safely, providing he did not turn again and land on his head instead of his feet. It was a chance very liable to happen, as he knew from his experience of a second before.

They heard him coming, but did not catch the significance of it.

"What's that!" exclaimed Bluff, springing up in alarm.

"I don -- "

"Y-e-o-w!"

Tad had uttered the shrill scream. With great presence of mind he hoped to take them so by surprise that they would hesitate for the few seconds, and that in this delay he would be able to get away.

The lad's feet struck the ground, his body plunged forward and he fell sprawling at the very feet of the men he was seeking to get away from.

"Catch him! It's a man!" roared the leader.

With one accord they sprang for the prostrate form of Tad Butler.

CHAPTER IX

TAD OUTWITS HIS PURSUERS

Tad was lithe and supple. As the champion wrestler of the high school, back in his home town in Missouri, he was possessed of many tricks that had proved useful to him on more than one occasion since the Pony Riders set out on their summer's jaunt.

"Y-e-o-w!" yelled the lad in a high-pitched, piercing voice, intended to confuse his enemy. And it served its purpose well.

As the men leaped upon him, Tad raised himself to all fours, his back slightly arched. In this position he ran on hands and feet like a monkey, darting straight between the legs of the man with the beard.

The big man flattened himself on the ground face downward, while Tad, who had tripped him, was well outside the ring. In an instant the leader's fellows had dropped on him and the four men were floundering helplessly, in what, to all appearances, might have been a football scrimmage.

Tad was not yelling now. He was fairly flying, running on his toes and seeking to do so without making the slightest sound.

The men quickly untangled themselves and with yells of rage bounded from their camp in search of the one who had caused so much disturbance. It had all happened so quickly that they had not succeeded in getting a good look at their tormentor.

"It's a boy!" roared Bluff. "Catch him. No, shoot! Don't let him get away!"

"Where is he!"

"I don't know. Fan the bushes, fan everything. We've got to get him!"

"Keep it up. Do you see him?"

"No."

As Tad heard the bullets snipping the leaves over his head, he instinctively ducked and, turning sharply to the left, skulked through the trees. By the flickering light of the camp fire he had seen something that gave him a sudden idea.

"Watch out. There he is?"

"Where, where?"

"There, by the ponies. Give it to him!" cried Jake.

"Stop, you fools!" thundered the leader. "Do you want to kill the bronchs? Get after him. What are you standing there like a lot of dumbheads for?"

"I see him. I kin pink him," yelled one of the four.

"I said go after him. Not a shot in that direction!" commanded Bluff.

Tad bad caught a glimpse of the ponies.

"I'm going to try it," he breathed.

No thought of wrong entered his mind. He was about to take a horse that did not belong to him. He knew his life was at stake and that having overheard their plans he would be sure to suffer were he to fall into their hands.

"It's not stealing. It's just fighting them on their own ground," gasped the boy, tugging desperately at the stake rope in an effort to free the first pony he came to.

The leash resisted all his efforts.

Out came the lad's jack knife. One sweep and the rope fell apart. They had discovered him. Every second was precious now. He was thankful that the men had removed neither bridles nor saddles, though he knew the bit was hanging from the animal's mouth.

But Tad cared little for this. He could manage the pony, he felt sure. With a yell of defiance he leaped into the saddle and dug his fist into the animal's side, uttering a shrill, "yip-yip!"

The pony, responding to the demands of its rider, sprang away through the forest, putting the lad in imminent peril of being swept off by low hanging limbs.

"He's getting away. He's got one of the ponies. Give it

to him now, but don't hit the rest of the cayuses!" yelled the leader in high excitement.

Tad had it in mind to liberate the other animals and start them off on a stampede. It was the fault of the outlaw cowboys that he did not. They discovered his whereabouts sooner than he had hoped they might. It was all he could do to get one pony free and mount in time, for they were running toward him at top speed.

Instantly, upon their leader giving them the order to fire, the men raised their weapons, taking quick, careful aim, and pulled the triggers.

Their bullets whistled far above the head of the fleeing boy, as the ground was sloping and he was traveling downward rapidly.

"Keep it up. You may get in a chance shot. No, stop. Take to the ponies."

Three of them, including the leader, cast loose the remaining animals, and springing upon their backs, spurred the bronchos into a run. They were in hot pursuit of the lad now, with freshly loaded guns ready to fire the instant they came within range of him.

Tad's pony was crashing through the brush, making such a racket that there could be no trouble about their keeping on the trail. They needed no light by which to follow it unerringly.

The boy soon came to a realization of this. Then again the men were so much more familiar with mountain riding that he felt sure they would eventually overhaul him. Even now they were gaining. There could be no doubt of that.

"I'll ride as long as I can, then I'll try to get away from them some other way," he decided.

The moment was rapidly approaching when he would be forced to resort to other tactics. Just what these should be he did not know. He would either be shot or captured in the event of his being unable to devise some other method of escape.

Tad Butler was resourceful. He had no idea of giving up yet. He was determined above all, to defeat the desperate purpose of these men and save Mr. Simms from the loss of his flock.

"We're gaining on him!" cried one of the pursuers. "I can hear the pony plainer now."

"Yes, I kin hear him snort," added another.

"You'll hear that cub doing some snorting on his own account in a minute," snarled Bluff, applying the spurs mercilessly.

"Shall we shoot, Cap!"

"I'll let you know when to shoot. No use filling all the trees in the range full of lead. We'll be up with him in a few minutes now and there'll be things doing. He can't get away. We've got him to rights this time."

"He's a slick one whoever he is. Think he heard us?"

"Can't guess. Don't make any difference anyhow. He won't have a chance to use the information, if he did hear."

"We're coming up on him," cried Jake.

"Halt!" bellowed the leader.

The pony in the lead did not slacken its speed in the least.

Bluff repeated his command, but still without perceptible result.

"Halt or we shoot!"

Tad Butler made no reply. He was leaning far over on the pony's neck now. In this position he was less likely to be swept off by limbs, and, again, were they to fire on him as they had threatened, there was a much better chance of the shots going harmlessly over, instead of through him. Thus far their marksmanship had been poor.

This was the second time the lad had been under fire, the first having been in the battle of the mountaineers, when the Pony Riders were in the Rocky Mountains, on which occasion Tad had conducted himself with such coolness and bravery.

Tad realized no fear, however. It thrilled him. A strange sense of elation possessed him. He felt strong and resourceful - he felt that he would be willing to do or dare almost anything.

"Let him have it!" commanded the leader sternly.

The men obeyed instantly.

Their weapons sent a rattling fire in the direction of the fleeing broncho.

"Halt! Will you halt!"

The pony still plunged on.

"Once more!"

The men fired again, two rounds each.

This time they heard the pony plunge crashing to the ground. His rapid course had come to a sudden end.

The pursuers set up a yell of triumph.

"He's down! He's down! We've got him!"

"Give him another one!"

To make sure that their man should not escape they fired their weapons again.

The pursuers dashed up with drawn revolvers, ready to shoot at the least sign of resistance.

Bluff leaped from his pony and struck a match.

Tad's mount lay dying in the brush.

"There's no one here," said Bluff, his face working nervously.

Of Tad Butler there was no sign. He had disappeared utterly.

CHAPTER X

THE RIDE FOB HELP

"There's Pink-eye!" exclaimed Ned Rector.

"Is it possible?" answered the Professor. "Then something has happened to Tad."

"Mebby - mebby the bear's got him," suggested Stacy Brown, his face blanching.

All through the night the little party had sat up anxiously awaiting the return of their companion, who had set out after the bear. The tent had been ruined, but they found that the rifles had not been harmed at all, having been stacked in front of the small tents.

Early in the morning the three boys and Professor Zepplin had followed Tad's trail for some distance into the foothills, but feared to penetrate too far for fear of getting lost. The Professor reasoned that it would be much better to return to camp and give Tad a chance to find his way in in case he himself should prove to have been lost.

This the boys had done, but they were impatient to be doing something more active. Ned Rector was fairly fuming, because their guardian would not permit him to set out alone in search of the missing boy.

"No," the Professor had said; "if I did that with all of you, we should have the whole party scattered over the mountains and it is doubtful if we should all get together again before snow flies."

Yet when Tad's pony came trotting back to camp, the matter took on a more serious aspect. Something must be done and at once.

"Now, will you let me go, Professor?" begged Ned.

"Not in those mountains alone, if that is what you mean."

"Then what can we do?"

"If the guide were only here!" interjected Walter. "Do you suppose I could find him?"

"It will be useless to try, my boy. About the only course we can follow now, is that leading back to Forsythe, and I am not sure that we shouldn't be lost doing that."

"Then we don't know it," retorted Ned. "I know the trail. I could go back over it with my eyes shut. Why would that not be the idea, Professor? Why not let me ride back to Forsythe? Mr. Simms would give us some one who knew the foothills and mountains and I could bring him back."

"Let me see, how far is it?" mused the Professor.

"Thirty miles, he said."

"Why, it would take you couple of days to make that and back."

"You try me and see. I can get a fresh pony to come back with, and if I do not return with the guide, what difference does it make? He's the one you want. But never fear, I'll be back with him between now and morning if I have no bad luck," urged the lad earnestly.

"I am half inclined to agree to your plan. If I were sure that you knew the way -- "

"It is not possible to get lost. We have the compasses and we know the direction in which Forsythe lies. All we have to do is to travel in an opposite direction from that by which we came."

"Supposing we all go!" suggested Walter.

"Wouldn't do at all," answered the Professor, with an emphatic shake of the head. "Some one must remain here in case Tad returns. That boy will get back somehow. I feel sure of that. He is resourceful and strong. And besides, he has my revolver. No; more than one on the trip would be apt to delay rather than to help. Master Ned, you may go." "Good!" shouted the lad. Bad-eye looked up almost resentfully as the boy approached him on the run, threw on the saddle and cinched the girths.

The hits were slipped into the animal's mouth, and, placing his left foot in the stirrup, Ned threw himself into the saddle.

"I'm ready now," he said, his eyes sparkling with anticipation, as he rode up to the little group.

"I'll show you that I'm not a tenderfoot even if I am from Missouri," he laughed.

"Be careful," warned Professor Zepplin.

"Don't worry about me, and, Chunky, you look out for bears. If Tad should come in within the next half hour or so, you can fire off your rifles to let me know. Then I'll turn about and come back. Good-bye, all."

"Good-bye and good luck," they shouted.

Giving a gentle pressure to the spurs, Ned Rector started off on his long ride at a brisk gallop. Within a short time the lad had the satisfaction of finding that he was emerging from the foothills. He then pulled up the pony and consulted his compass. "Five points north of east. The Professor said that should take me back. Besides I remember that we came this way yesterday. I'm going to save some time by fording that fork without going the roundabout way we took before."

Ned galloped on again. Had it not been for his anxiety over Tad, he would have enjoyed his ride to the fullest. The morning was glorious; the sun had not yet risen high enough to make the heat uncomfortable; birds were singing and in spots where the sun had not yet penetrated a heavy dew was glistening on foliage and grass.

Ned drew a long breath, drinking in the delicious air.

"This is real," he said. "Nothing artificial about this. I wish I might stay here always."

The lad did not think of the deep snows and biting cold

of the northern winters there, winters so severe that hundreds of head of sheep and cattle frequently perished from the killing weather. He saw nature only in her most peaceful mood.

He had ridden on for something more than two hours, when he came to the East Fork, where they had had such an exciting experience two nights before. After a few moments' riding along the bank he discovered the spot where they had made their camp on the opposite side.

"I'm going to take a chance and ford right here," he decided. "No, I guess my mission is too important to take the risk. If I should get caught in there I should at least be delayed. There's somebody else who must be considered. That's Tad."

Half a mile above, the lad found a place that he felt safe in trying. Luckily he got across without mishap. He had found a rocky bar without being aware of it, and the water while swift was shallow enough so that by slipping his feet from the stirrups and holding them up, he was able to ford the stream without even getting them damp.

"I wonder why we didn't find this place the other night," he said aloud. "I guess we were in too big a hurry. That's the trouble with us boys. We blunder along without using our heads. But, I guess I had better not boast until after I have gotten back safely from Forsythe," he laughed. "I may need some good advice myself before that is accomplished."

The pony with ears laid back had settled to a long, loping gallop, covering mile after mile without seeming to feel the strain in the least.

Some distance beyond the Fork, Ned descried a horseman who had halted on beyond him, evidently awaiting his approach.

Ned was not greatly concerned about this. On the contrary, it was a relief to see a human being.

The man hailed him as he drew up. Ned noted the red beard and the general sinister appearance of the man.

"How," greeted the stranger, tossing his hand to the lad.

"How," answered Ned in kind.

"Where you headed!"

"Forsythe."

"Stranger in these parts, I reckon?"

"Yes, sir."

"On a herd?"

"Expect to he soon. Just finished a drive down in Texas."

"Cattle, of course?"

"Oh, yes."

"That's right. This sheep business has got to stop. I hear there's going to be something doing round these parts pretty lively," grinned the stranger.

"What do you mean?" asked the lad, peering sharply into the man's face.

"Oh, nothing much," answered the other. "Thought being as you were a cowman it might interest you some."

"It does," replied the boy almost sharply.

"Well, guess the rest, then," laughed the stranger. "Where'd you get that pony?"

"Is that not rather a personal question?" asked Ned, smiling coldly.

"Not in this country. Kinder reminded me of a nag that belonged to me. He strayed away from my ranch a few weeks ago," said the fellow significantly.

"It wasn't this pony," retorted Ned, flushing. "I bought this animal. Good day, sir, I must be getting along."

"In a hurry, ain't ye?"

"I am," answered Ned, touching the spurs to the pony's sides and galloping off.

"Hey, hold on a minute," called the stranger.

"Can't. In too much of a hurry," replied Ned.

"I don't like the looks of that fellow at all," muttered the boy as he rode on, instinctively urging his mount along at an increased speed to put as much distance as possible between himself and the curious stranger.

"Funny he should ask me that question about my pony. However, perhaps it is a peculiarity in this part of the country. Wonder what he meant by saying that there would be something doing here pretty quick."

After a time Ned turned in his saddle and looked back. The horseman was standing as Ned had left him. He was watching the boy. Ned swung his hand, and then turned, glad that he was well rid of the man.

Late in the afternoon, he saw the village of Forsythe just ahead of him. The boy could have shouted at the sight.

"Straight as you could shoot a bullet," he chuckled. "I guess I can follow the old Custer trail without getting lost.

He did not pause, but galloped on into the village and up the main street, not halting until he had reached the bank with which Mr. Simms was connected.

He was stiff and sore from the long, continuous ride, and as he dismounted he found that he could scarcely stand.

After tethering the pony to the iron rod that had been fastened to two posts, Ned walked into the bank. Red-faced and dusty he presented himself to the banker. At first the latter did not appear to recognize him.

"I am Ned Rector of the Pony Rider Boys," explained the lad.

Mr. Simms sprang up and grasped the boy cordially by the hand.

"This is a surprise. You back so soon? Why, is anything wrong!"

"Well, yes, there is," admitted Ned.

"Sit down and tell me about it."

Ned seated himself, but the effort hurt him and he winced a little.

"Stiffened up, eh? Where did you come from?"

The lad explained and Mr. Simms uttered a soft whistle.

"Well, you have had a ride. I didn't suppose you boys could ride like that. I suppose the guide found you?"

"We have seen nothing of him at all."

"Is it possible? I should not have troubled myself to come back to tell you had it not been for the fact that one of our boys is lost."

"Lost?"

"Yes. At least we think so. He has been away since early last evening. We should not have worried so much had not his pony returned without him early this morning. We dared not go far into the mountains to search for him for fear of getting lost ourselves."

"You don't mean it?"

"Yes. I came back to see if you could give me a man from here, or get me one rather. One who knows the mountains and who will ride back with me at once."

"Of course I will. You did perfectly right in coming to me quickly. My foreman is in town to-day. He will be in shortly and I think he will know of some one who will answer your purpose. I wish you had ridden to my ranch, however. It would have been much nearer."

"I didn't know where it was."

"Of course not."

"While waiting for the foreman, tell me about how it all happened?" urged Mr. Simms.

Ned went over the events of the previous evening, in detail, to all of which the banker gave an attentive ear.

Mr. Simms regarded him with serious face.

"You young men are having plenty of excitement, I must say. Yes, you are right. Something must have happened to Master Tad. He looks to me like a boy who could be relied upon to look out for himself pretty well, however," added the banker.

"He is. We were afraid that perhaps he might have gotten into trouble with the bear."

"Quite likely. Do you plan on going back with the guide that we get for you?"

"Certainly."

"Then you will need a fresh, pony. I will have one brought around for you when you are ready to start. I should think, however, that it would be best for you to remain over until tomorrow. You'll be lamed up for sure."

"No, I must go back. I'll be lame all right, but it won't be the first time. I'm lame and sore now. I've polished that saddle so you could skate on it already," laughed Ned.

Mr. Simms laughed.

"I can understand that quite easily. I've been in the saddle a good share of my life, too. There comes the foreman now."

The foreman of the Simms ranch, who bore the euphonious name of Luke Larue, was a product of the West. Six feet tall, straight, muscular, with piercing gray eyes that looked out at one from beneath heavy eyelashes, Ned instinctively recognized him as a man calculated to inspire confidence.

He shook hands with the young man cordially, sweeping him with a quick, comprehensive glance.

Mr. Simms briefly related all that Ned Rector had told him, and the foreman glanced at the young man with renewed interest after learning of the ride he had taken that morning.

"Pretty good for a tenderfoot, eh?"

Ned's bronzed face took on a darker hue as he blushed violently.

"I don't exactly call myself that now, sir," he replied.

"Right. You say your friend chased a bear out!"

The lad nodded.

Luke shook his head.

"Bad. Can he shoot?"

"Oh, yes. But he had only a revolver - a heavy thirty-eight calibre that belongs to Professor Zepplin."

"Nice toy to hunt bears with," laughed the foreman. "Bear's probably cleaned him up. I'll get a man I know and I'll go back with you myself. We can run down the trail easily enough, but it will need two trailers, one to follow the pony and the other the bear after their trails separate," the foreman informed them wisely.

"Do - do - you think he has been killed?" stammered Ned.

"I ain't saying. It looks bad, that's all."

Ned forced a composure that he did not feel. He started to ask a further question, when there came a sudden interruption that brought all three to their feet.

CHAPTER XI

A RACE AGAINST TIME

But to return to Tad and his experiences in seeking to elude his pursuers. The boy saw that it was a question of a few moments only before they would surely overhaul him. Already the bullets from their revolvers were making their presence known about him.

"Getting too warm for me," decided the lad coolly.

It occurred to him to leave the pony and take his chances on foot. The animal did not belong to him and he would have to abandon it sooner or later.

A volley closer than the rest emphasized his decision. The lad freed his feet from the stirrups and slipped from the saddle, at the same time giving the pony a sharp slap, uttering a shrill little "yip!" as the animal dashed away.

After this, Tad did not wait a second. He ran obliquely away from the pony. This he thought would be better than turning sharply to the left or right. The next moment he came into violent contact with the base of a tree. He noted that it's trunk was a sloping one, and without pausing to think of the wisdom of his act, the lad quickly scrambled up it.

To his delight he found himself amid the spreading branches of a pinon tree. He wriggled in among the foliage, stretching himself along a limb, where he clung almost breathless. He had no sooner gained that position than the pony went down under the fire of his pursuers.

"Too bad," muttered Tad. "It's a shame I had to desert the broncho. He did me a good service."

The men galloped by a few feet from the boy's hiding place and came to a halt beside the prostrate pony. His straining ears caught their every word.

When they began to shoot, Tad flattened himself still more, instinctively. Some of the bullets passed close beneath him, and he wished that he might have chosen a higher tree in which to hide.

Bang!

It seemed to have cut the leaves just behind his head.

Tad repressed a shiver and shut his lips tightly together. He was determined not to permit himself to feel any fear.

At last the men joined each other right under the tree in which he was hiding. Tad fairly held his breath.

"Well, what do you think, Cap?"

"Don't think. I know. The cayuse has given us the slip."

"No, not much use looking for him. Better wait here

till morning then try to trail him down, if we don't find him laid out somewhere in the bushes round here," suggested one.

"Yes, we might as well go back to camp. We can't spend much time looking for him in the morning. We've got other work to do. I wish I knew just how much that fellow overheard. Queerest thing I ever come across, and I don't like it a little bit."

They removed the saddle and bridle from the dead pony, after which they started slowly away.

Tad breathed again. Yet he still lay along the pinon limb, every sense on the alert. He was not sure that it was not a trick to draw him out. He already was too good a woodsman to be caught napping thus easily.

After a time, however, deciding that all the men had left, the lad cautiously began to work his way down the sloping tree trunk. His feet touched the ground, his arms still being about the pinon trunk. In that position he lay for several minutes.

"I guess it's all right," decided Tad, straightening up. "The question is, which way shall I go? I've got to be a long ways from here by daylight or that will be the end of me. It would be just my luck to run right into that gang again."

After pondering a moment he decided that, knowing the direction the men had taken, there was only one thing for him to do. He would strike out in the opposite direction.

He did so at once, first standing in one spot for some

time to get his bearings exactly. Then, the lad started away bravely. At first he moved cautiously and as he got further away, increased his speed and went on with less caution.

He kept bearing to the right to offset the natural tendency to stray too far the other way, which is usual with those who are lost in the forest.

Tad was tired and sore, but he did not allow himself to give any thought to that. His one thought now, was to get out of the forest and give the alarm to the owner of the ranch against whom he had heard the men plotting.

Hearing water running somewhere near, Tad realized that he was very thirsty, and after a few minutes' search, he located a small mountain stream. Making a cup of his hands he drank greedily, then took up his weary journey again. Forcing his way through dense patches of brush, stumbling into little gullies, becoming entangled amongst fallen trees and rotting brush heaps, boy and clothes suffered a sad beating.

Day dawned faintly after what had seemed an endless night. The sky which he could faintly make out through the trees above him, was of a dull leaden gray, which slowly merged into an ever deepening blue. Off to his right he caught glimpses of patches of blue that were lower down.

"I must be up in the mountains," said Tad aloud. "I wonder how I ever got up here."

This was a certain aid to him, however. He reasoned that if the valley lay to his right, he must be going nearly northward. That would lead him toward the place where he believed the Simms ranch lay, and at the present moment that was Tad Butler's objective point. It might be losing valuable time were he to try to find his way back to camp.

"I'll get down lower," he decided, turning sharply to the right and descending the sloping side of the mountains.

Reaching the lower rocks, he found that he was more likely to lose his way there than higher up. He was now in the foothills. There, all sense of direction was lost. So Tad, began ascending the mountain. He went up just far enough to enable him to see the blue sky off to the right again, after which he forced his way along the rocky slope. It was tough traveling and he felt it in every muscle of his body.

After plodding on for hours, he paused finally and listened.

"Thought I heard a bell tinkle," he muttered. "I've heard of people hearing such things when they were nearly crazed with hunger and fatigue on the desert. I wonder if I am going the same way. Oh, pshaw! Tad Butler, you could keep on walking all day. Don't be silly," he said to himself encouragingly.

The tinkling bell was now a certainty.

"I know what it is!" exclaimed the lad joyously. "It's sheep! I've heard them before. I'm near sheep and that means there will be men around. It's sheepmen that I am looking for now."

With hat in hand, the boy dashed off down the

mountain side, leaping lightly from rock to rock, his red neck-handkerchief streaming in the breeze behind him, as he followed an oblique course toward the foothills.

All at once he burst out on to a broad, green mesa, and there, before his delighted eyes was a great herd of snowy-white sheep grazing contentedly. Off on the further side of the flock he descried a man lazily sitting in his saddle while a dog was rounding up a bunch of stray lambs further to Tad's right.

The man was watching the work of the dog, so that he did not discover the lad at once.

Tad decided that he would go around the herd to the left. That appeared to be the shortest way to reach him. He did not wish to try to go straight through the herd.

He had gone but a little way before he saw that the man had observed him and was now riding around the upper end of the flock to meet him.

"Hello, what do you want?" shouted the fellow.

"I want to find Mr. Simms's ranch. Is it anywhere near here?"

"Two miles up that way. Where'd you come from?"

"I don't know. I've been lost in the mountains. I must see Mr. Simms at once."

"Guess you've got a long walk ahead of you then," laughed the sheepman. "Boss Simms is up to Forsythe."

"Is his family at the ranch?" asked Tad.

"I reckon the women folks is. You seem to be in a hurry, pardner."

"I am. I must hurry."

Wondering at the haste of the disreputable looking youngster, the sheepman watched him until he had gotten out of sight. Finding the footing good and encouraged by the knowledge that he had but two miles to go, the lad dropped into a lope which he kept up until the white side of the Simms ranch buildings reflected back the morning sun just ahead of him.

Tads legs almost collapsed under him as he staggered into the yard and asked a boy whom he saw there, for Mrs. Simms.

He was directed by a wave of the hand to a near-by door, on which Tad rapped insistently.

"I wish to see Mrs. Simms, please," he said to the servant, who responded to his knock.

"I am Mrs. Simms. What is it you wish?" answered a voice somewhere in the room. It was a pleasant voice, reminding Tad much of his mother's, and a sense of restfulness possessed him almost at once. He felt almost as if he were at home again.

"I would like to speak with you, alone, please."

"Who are you?"

"I am Tad Butler from Missouri. I -- "

"Oh, yes, nay husband told me you were expected," she said cordially, extending her hand.

"I owe you an apology for appearing in this shape, but I have been lost in the mountains and seem to be rather badly in need of a change of clothes," smiled the lad.

"Come right in. Never mind the clothes. Perhaps I may be able to help you. You say you have been lost?"

"Yes."

"Where are your companions?"

"I don't know. I left them in camp somewhere, I am not sure where."

"Oh, that is too bad. If you will remain until night perhaps we can spare one of the herders to help you find them -- "

"Pardon me, but it is not for that that I came here," interrupted the lad. "It was on a far more important matter."

"Yes?"

"It is a matter that concerns your husband very seriously."

"Tell me about it, please?" said Mrs. Simms anxiously.

"Have you anyone that you could send to Forsythe at once with an urgent message for your husband?" he asked.

"There is no one. The herders would not dare to leave their flocks - that is not until the sheep were safe in their corral to-night."

"That will be too late. I'll have to go myself. Have you a spare pony that I could ride!"

"Of course. That is if you can rope one out of the pen and saddle it yourself."

"Certainly. I can do that," said the boy quickly. "But I shall probably ride him pretty hard and fast. I do not think Mr. Simms will object when he learns my reasons."

"Is it so serious as that?"

"It seems so to me. Last night while lost in the mountains I overheard some men plotting against your husband. They said he was expecting a large number of sheep that were being brought in on a drive."

"Yes, that is true."

"They were planning to attack the herd, to stampede it and kill all the animals they could -- "

"Is it possible?" demanded the woman, growing pale.

"They mean it, too. I think I will get the pony and start now," decided Tad, rising.

"You are a brave boy," exclaimed the banker's wife, laying an impulsive hand on Tad's shoulder. "I wish you did not have to go. You are tired out now. I can see that."

"I'll be all right when I get in the saddle again," he smiled. "Thank you just as much."

"You shall not leave this house until you have had your breakfast. What can I be thinking of?" announced Mrs. Simms. "You are doing us all a very great service and I am not even thoughtful enough to offer you something to eat though you are half starved."

"I had better not spare the time to sit down," objected Tad. "I must be going if you will show me the way."

"Not until you have eaten."

"Then, will you please make me some sandwiches? I can eat them in the saddle, and I shall get along very nicely until I get to town. I'll eat enough to make up for lost time when I get at it," he laughed.

He was out of the house and running toward the corral, to which Mrs. Simms had directed him. Tad hunted about until he found a rope; then going to the enclosure scanned the ponies critically.

"I think I'll take that roan," he decided. "Looks as if he had some life in him."

The roan had plenty, as Tad soon learned. However, after a lively little battle he succeeded in getting the animal from the enclosure and saddling and bridling him.

Tad could find no spurs, but he helped himself to a crop which he found in the stable, though, from what he had been able to observe, the pony would require little urging to make him go at a good speed.

Mrs. Simms was outside when Tad rode up. She had prepared a lunch for him, placing it in a little leather bag with a strap attached for fastening the package over his shoulder.

"Please say nothing about what I have told you," urged Tad. "I don't want them to know we understand their plans. That is the only way Mr. Simms will be able to catch them."

"Of course, I shall not mention it. Good-bye and good luck."

Tad mounted his broncho and was off, head-ding directly for the town of Forsythe.

CHAPTER XII

A TIMELY WARNING

Arriving in the little town about noon, Tad dashed up the street toward Mr. Simms' bank. Tethering his broncho to the post, he entered the bank, and in his anxiety, pushed open the door of Mr. Simms' private office without ceremony.

Here, as we already know, were Mr. Simms, Luke Larue and Ned, all eagerly discussing Tad's mysterious disappearance. For a moment not one of those in the office spoke a word. Tad stood before them, his clothes hanging in ribbons, his face scratched and torn, the dust and grime of the plains fairly ground into his face, hands and neck.

Luke Larue, of course, did not know the lad, but the keen eyes of the banker lighted up with recognition.

"Master Ned," he said. "I think if this young man were washed and dressed up, you might recognize in him the friend you are looking for."

"Tad!" exclaimed the boy, springing forward, excitedly grasping the hands of the freckle-faced boy.

"Hello, Ned. What you doing here?'

"Looking for you. They're all upset back at the camp. We thought the bear had gotten you."

"No, I got the bear. A two-legged bear nearly got me later on. I'll tell you all about it later. I want to see Mr. Simms now."

"Master Tad, I don't know where you have been, but you certainly look used up. This is the foreman of my ranch, Mr. Luke Larue," said the banker.

With a quiet smile on the face of each, man and boy shook hands.

"Heard about you," greeted Luke. "Heard you was a tenderfoot. Don't look like it."

"Neither do I feel like it. Feel as if I'd been put through an ore mill or something that would grind equally fine. When do you expect the sheep?"

The foreman shot a keen glance at him.

"To-day or to-morrow. Why?"

"Because there is trouble ahead for you when they get here."

"What do you mean?"

"What is this you say?" demanded Mr. Simms.

"That is what I have come here to tell you about. There is a plan on foot to ride down your sheep when they get here."

Larue laughed.

"Guess they'd better not try it. Where did you hear that fairy story, young man?"

"It's not a fairy tale - it is the fact."

Mr. Simms had risen from his chair and was now facing Tad. He saw in the lad's face what convinced him that there was more to be told.

"Let me hear all about it, Master Tad," he said.

"Somebody's been filling the boy up with tenderfoot yarns," smiled the foreman.

Tad did not appear to heed the foreman's scoffing. Instead, he began in a low incisive voice the narration of his experiences of the previous night, beginning with the bear hunt and ending with his finding his way out of the forest that morning.

As he proceeded with the story, the lines on the face of the banker grew tense, his blue eyes appearing to fade to a misty gray.

At first indifferent, Larue soon pricked up his ears, then became intensely interested in the story.

"And that's about all I can think of to tell you," concluded Tad.

Ned uttered a low whistle of amazement.

"So you think this is a tenderfoot yarn, eh?" asked the banker, turning to his foreman.

"Not now," answered Larue. "I guess the boy did get it straight."

"Humph! You had no means of knowing - didn't hear what his name was, did you?"

"No, sir. He was a big man with red hair and beard and he had a scar over his left temple. The men with him called him Bluff."

"Don't know any such man, do you, Luke?"

Luke shook his head.

"Nobody who would mix up in such a dirty deal as that. Oscar Stillwell who owns a cow ranch on the other side of the Rosebud, answers to that description, but he ain't the man for that kind of a raw job. Known him five years now."

"Sure about him, are you?"

"Positive. He don't approve of the hatred that the cow-men generally have for the sheep business. Says there's free grass enough for all of us and that the sheepmen have just as much right to it as the cowmen. I'll ride over to his ranch this afternoon and talk with him. I can tell him the story without his giving it away."

"Just as you think best. You know your man and I don't."

"Yes. And if there's any such plan on foot, he'll be likely to know about it."

"This business has been getting altogether too

common. All the way up and down the old Custer trail, there has been sheep killing, sheep stealing, stampeding and no end of trouble for the past year. We have seemed unable to fix the responsibility on anyone. But I'll tell you that if they try to break into any of our herds this time, somebody is going to be shot," decided Mr. Simms, compressing his lips tightly together. "We're forewarned this time."

"Have you any suggestions, Mr. Simms? I must be getting back to the ranch if this is in the wind?"

"Yes. Let no one outside of our own men, know that we suspect, unless it be Stillwell and you are sure you can trust him -- "

"There's no doubt of it."

"When the new herd gets here, put all the men on it save one who will watch the corral at night. They won't be likely to attack the sheep that are in the enclosure. It's the new ones that we have to herd on the open range that they will be likely to direct their efforts toward. Master Tad has heard as much."

"Will you be out?"

"Of course. I'll ride out this afternoon and remain at the ranch or on the range until this thing has blown over. We had better begin grazing north at once. I want to get them up where the grass is better, as soon as possible. Then you can let them take their time until after shearing. We're late with that as it is. See that the men are well armed, but make no plans until I have been out and looked the ground over."

"Very well. Suppose you have no idea where it was that these men found you, or where you found them?" asked the foreman.

"No, sir. I was too busy to take notice."

"I should say so," laughed Mr. Simms.

"I'd better be moving then, if there's nothing else to be said," decided Luke.

"I think you had better spare the time to take these young men back to their camp."

"I helped myself to one of your horses, Mr. Simms. The roan."

"Help yourself to anything that belongs to me, young man," answered the banker. "You have done us a service that nothing we can do will repay."

"The roan - you say you rode the roan?" asked Lame.

"Yes. He's a good one."

"Did he throw you?"

"He tried to," grinned Tad.

"Then I take back all I said about your being a tenderfoot. There aren't three men on the ranch who can stick on his back when he takes a notion that he doesn't want them to."

"Luke, I have asked these young men to join our outfit. When I did so, I didn't know I was drawing a prize.

They rather thought the sheep business wouldn't suit them, having been out with a herd of cows -- "

"We shall be glad to accept your kind offer, Mr. Simms," interrupted Tad. "I've changed my mind since I saw how the cattle men act toward sheep."

"That's good."

"When do you wish us to join you?"

"Join to-day by all means, if you have no other plans. I am surprised that the guide failed you. You will not need a guide if you go with the outfit, and you can take as many side trips for hunting, as you wish."

"That will be fine," agreed Ned Rector.

"Another idea occurs to me. My boy Philip has not been well, and if you lads have no objection, I should like to send him along with the herd. If you will keep an eye on him to see that he doesn't get into trouble, I shall be deeply grateful to you."

"Of course we shall," answered Tad brightening. "How old is he?"

"Only twelve. He's quite a baby still. You will not have any responsibility at all, you understand. He and Old Hicks the cook of the outfit, are great friends, and Hicks will look after him most of the time."

"We shall be glad to have him with us," glowed Ned.

"Perhaps you would prefer not to join until after this trouble is over. It probably would be safer, come to think of it -- "

"No. I think we should like to join right away," interrupted Tad hastily. "Besides, we may be able to be of some service to you. We can handle cattle, so I don't know why we should not be of use with sheep. Don't you think so, Ned?"

"Yes, of course. That will just suit Chunky, too. That's what we call our friend Stacy Brown," explained Ned, with a grin. "He's the fat boy, you know."

"Was once. He's getting over it rapidly," laughed Tad. "His uncle won't know him when he gets back to Chillicothe."

"You have had most of the fun and excitement thus far, Tad. Now the rest of us want to have some too."

"If you call being shot at fun, then I have had more than my share."

"Most likely you will have all that's coming to you if this thing comes off," grunted the foreman. "I'm going out now. Meet you here in an hour. We'll ride back to the ranch. I'll either accompany you to your own camp from there, or send some one else who knows the way. I think I understand where your friends are located. I'm going to get a case of shells at the hardware store, Mr. Sirnms."

"That's the idea. Better take out some more guns while you are about it. You know what to buy."

At the appointed time Larue presented himself at the bank, announcing himself as ready for the ride. The banker again renewed his expressions of appreciation of all that Tad Butler had done for him, after which they swung into their saddles and started off on their long ride over the plains.

There was plenty of excitement before the Pony Riders. Their few weeks with the herd were to be more eventful, even, than had been their journey with the cattle over the plains of Texas.

CHAPTER XIII

PREPARING FOR AN ATTACK

It was late on the following forenoon when the Pony Rider Boys descended on the Simms ranch, bag and baggage. Larue had relieved one of the herders and sent him back with Tad Butler and Ned Rector, to bring up the rest of the party.

The parlor tent they found had been too badly damaged to be worth carrying along, so they left it where the bear had wrecked it.

"Heard anything from the herd?" was Tad's first question as Mr. Simms came out to greet them.

"We certainly have. They are within three miles of here now. I have given orders to keep them clear of the ranch, and the herders are at work deflecting them to the northward. We shall bed them down about five miles from here to-night. To-morrow we will push on slowly for the grass regions up the state. I have arranged for you to remain at the ranch to-night."

"Oh, no. We prefer to go out and join the herd," objected Tad.

"We most certainly do," added Ned. "That's what we

are here for."

"Have you heard anything new?" asked Tad, in a low voice, leaning from his saddle.

"Yes. I heard that the cowmen all through here are stirred up. It isn't any one man or set of men that's doing it. We have received threats from different sources if we allow the sheep to stray from our own ranch," answered Mr. Simms, with serious face.

"And you have decided -- ?"

"To go on."

"Hello, is this your son, Philip?" asked Tad, as a slender, pale-faced boy came toward them.

"Yes, this is Phil. Come here, Phil and meet my young friends."

The Pony Rider Boys took to the lad at once. He was a manly little fellow, but delicate to the point of being fragile, the lad having only recently recovered from a serious attack of typhoid fever.

"You see what the outdoor life has done for these young gentlemen, Phil," said Mr. Simms. "I shall expect you to come back this fall, looking every bit as well as they do now. All get ready for dinner. It will be served in a few moments. Later in the day, we shall move out on the range. Phil, have you packed up your things?"

"Yes, sir. I'm all ready."

The noon meal was a jolly affair. The herders cooked their own meals out on the range, and after this the boys would eat with them. But to-day they were invited guests in the home of the rancher and hanker. In the meantime Professor Zepplin and Mr. Simms had become interested in each other and already were looking forward to the next few days on the range together, with keen pleasure.

The start was made shortly after three o'clock, the party reaching their destination well before sundown.

The Pony Riders uttered a shout as they descried the white canvas top of the chuck wagon. It was a familiar sight to them. On beyond that was a perfect sea of white backs and bobbing heads, where the great herd was grazing contentedly after its long journey to the free grass of Montana. The boys had never seen anything like it.

The sheep dogs, too, were a source of never-ending interest. The boys watched the intelligent animals, as of their own accord they rounded up a bunch here and there that they had observed straying from the main herd, working the sheep back to their fellows quietly and without in the least appearing to disturb them.

"What kind of sheep is that over there?" asked Chunky, pointing.

"That's no sheep. That's Billy," answered Mr. Simms.

"Who's he?"

"The goat. You've no doubt heard of a bell wether?"

"I have," spoke up Tad.

"That's what Billy is. He leads the sheep. They will follow a leader almost anywhere. In crossing a stream Billy wades in without the least hesitation and they cross right over after him. Otherwise we should have great difficulty in getting them over."

"Oh, yes, I know a goat. Had one once," replied Stacy. "Does he butt?"

"Sometimes. His temper is not what might be called angelic. I suspect the boys have been teasing him pretty well. However, you want to look out for some of those rams. They are ugly and they can easily knock a man down. If you are up early in the morning you will see them at play - you will see what they can do with their tough heads."

"I forgot to tell you," said Larue in a low voice, "that some of the men report having encountered Indians during the day."

"That's nothing new. There are plenty of them around here," laughed the banker.

"They think they were Blackfeet. The reds were so far away, however, that the men could not make certain."

"Off the reservation again, eh? Probably think they can pick up a few sheep. Well, look out for them. If you catch them at any shines just shoot to scare. Don't hit them. We don't want any Government inquiry. I have suspected for a long time that some of them were hiding in the Rosebuds and that the Crow Indians were in league with them. It's only the bad Indians who stray from their reservations, you see," explained Mr. Simms. "We have to be on the lookout for these roving bands all the time or they'd steal all we have."

"I should think you would complain to the Indian agencies," suggested the Professor,

"Doesn't pay. They would take it out of us in a worse way, perhaps. They're a revengeful gang."

One by one the herders came in with their dogs and flocks, rounding the sheep in for the night, having chosen for the purpose a slight depression in the plain. For the first time, the boys had an opportunity to meet the ranchers and compare them with the cattle men they tad known in Texas. They were a hardy lot, taciturn and solemn-faced. The most silent man in the bunch, was Noisy Cooper, who scarcely ever spoke a word unless forced to do so by an insistent question. Bat Coyne had been a cattle man down in Texas, while Mary Johnson - so called because of his pink and white complexion, which no amount of sun or wind could tarnish - was said to have come from the East. He had left there for reasons best known to himself, working on sheep ever since.

It was Old Hicks, however, who interested Tad most. Hicks's first words after being introduced were in apology for being cook on a sheep ranch.

He was limping about, flourishing a frying-pan to accentuate his protests.

"I'm a cowpuncher, I am. Wish I'd never joined this mutton outfit," he growled.

"Then why did you?" asked Tad, smiling broadly.

"Why? I joined because I could get more pay. That's why. What you suppose I joined for?"

"I thought perhaps you preferred sheep," answered the lad meekly.

"Like them - like mutton?" snarled Old Hicks, hurling his frying-pan angrily into the chuck wagon. "Between sheep and had Injuns, give me the Injun every time. Why, every time I have to cook one it makes me sick; it does."

"Indians? Do you cook Indians?" asked Stacy, who had been an interested listener to the conversation.

"Wha - wha - cook Indians? No! I cook mutton. What do you take me for?"

"I - I - I didn't know," muttered Stacy meekly. "Thought I heard you say you did."

"You got another think coming," growled the cook, limping away. "Come over here and take a sniff at this kettle?" he called, turning back to Tad.

The lad did so.

"Smells fine, doesn't it?"

"I think so. What is it, mutton?"

"Boiled mutton. I kin smell the wool. Bah."

"Do you cook them with the wool on?" asked Chunky,

edging nearer the kettle.

"See here, young man. This here is a bad country to ask fool questions in. Use your eyes and ears. Give your tongue a rest. It'll stop on you some day."

Chunky retired somewhat crestfallen, and from that moment on he kept aloof from the irascible cook, whom he held in wholesome awe.

"Come and get it!" bellowed Old Hicks, who, after prodding about the interior of the kettle with a sharp stick for some time, decided that the hated mutton was ready to be served.

The Pony Riders did not share Hicks's repugnance to mutton. They helped themselves liberally, and even Phil Simms went so far as to pass his plate for a second helping. By the time the meal had been finished twilight was upon them.

The boys, when Professor Zepplin called their attention to the lateness of the hour, made haste to pitch their tents, while Mr. Simms, with Phil and the sheepmen, looked on approvingly.

"You boys go at it like troopers," he smiled. "You'll have to pitch your own, too, after to-day, Philip."

"We'll help him," chorused the boys. "We've got to do something to earn our board," said Ned.

"If we eat all the time the way we have tonight, there won't be many sheep left to graze by the time we've finished the trip," laughed Walter.

"Somebody has to eat the cook's share," interrupted Larue. "What I came over here to ask was whether you boys were intending to take your turns at herding for the next few nights?"

"Of course we are," they answered in one voice. "That's what we are up here for, "added Tad.

"Got any guns?"

"Rifles. Fortunately, they were not in the tent that was set afire by the bear, so they are all right," replied Tad. "However, I'll have to ask the Professor about taking them out. I do not think he will care to have us do so."

"I'll give you each a revolver," announced the foreman.

"Luke, never mind the guns. The boys will do their part by keeping guard. We don't want them to be mixed up in any trouble that may follow. If there is any shooting to be done, we can take care of that, I guess," said Mr. Simms, with a grim smile.

"Yes, I could not think of permitting it," said the Professor firmly; hence it was decided that the lads should go on as they had been doing, leaving the sterner work to those whose business it was to attend to it.

After the darkness had settled over the camp, the boys observed that there were more men present than had been the case when they had their supper.

Mr. Simms explained that they were some men he had sent for to help protect the herd. He had ordered them to report after dark, so that the trouble-makers might know nothing about the increased force. The rancher was determined to teach the cattle men of the free-grass range a lesson they would not soon forget.

"What do you wish us to do?" asked Walter. "We are anxious to get busy."

"I think two of you had better go out for the first half of the night; the other two for the latter half."

"Do we take our ponies?" asked Tad.

"Yes. All of us will ride, excepting the few men who are regularly on guard with the sheep. But you will not move around much. Make no noise and be watchful. That is all we can do."

It was decided that Ned and Walter should take the early trick; Tad and Stacy Brown going out after midnight.

The herders were already attending to their duties. And now Mr. Simms and the foreman having given their orders, the reserve force moved out one at a time until all had disappeared in the darkness. A signal had been agreed upon, so that they might recognize each other in the dark.

The rancher had thrown out his reserve force in the shape of a picket line, located some distance out from the herd and covering a circle something more than a mile in diameter. This was done so that in case of an attack they would have an opportunity to drive off their enemy without great danger to the herd. The battle, more than likely, would be ended before the cow-men could get near enough to the sheep to inflict any damage.

The two boys left camp rather closer together than had the others, as they were to keep in touch during their watch.

In a short time the guards were all placed and a great silence settled over the scene, broken only now and then by the bleating of a lamb that had lost its mother in the darkness.

CHAPTER XIV

BUNTED BY A MERINO RAM

The Simms outfit breathed a sigh of relief when daylight came again. There had been nothing more disturbing than Stacy Brown's yawns in the early part of the night.

So persistent had been these that the Professor and Mr. Simms found themselves yawning in sympathy. Old Hicks, who was sitting up to prepare hot coffee for any of the sheepmen who might come in, was affected in a like manner. Had it not been for the presence of the owner of the herd Hicks might have adopted heroic measures to put a stop to Stacy's yawns. As it was, he threatened all sorts of dire things. At breakfast time the cook seemed to be in a far worse humor than ever when he gave the breakfast call.

"Come and get it. And I hope it chokes you!" he bellowed, voicing his displeasure at everything and everybody in general.

Tad rode in as fresh as if he had not had a sleepless vigil. His rest of late had been more or less irregular, but it seemed to have not the slightest effect either on his spirits or his appetite.

All felt the relief from the strain of the night's watching and it was a more sociable company that gathered at the table than had been the case on the previous evening.

"Well, how do you like being a sheepman?" asked Mr. Simms jovially.

"It's better than being lost in the mountains and being shot at by cowmen," averred Tad.

"Perhaps you'll have a chance to enjoy the latter pleasure, still," said Mr. Simms. "I do not delude myself that we are out of danger yet; it may be that they have taken warning and given it up."

"What are the plans for to-day?" asked Ned Rector.

"The herd will graze on, and later in the day we shall move the camp five or six miles up the range. See any Indians last night?"

"No," answered the boys, sobering a little.

"Old Hicks is authority for the statement that they were hovering somewhere near during the night."

"How does he know?" asked Tad.

"You'll have to make inquiry of Hicks himself if you want to find out," laughed the rancher. "Probably the same way that he knows we are talking about him now."

All eyes were directed toward the cook.

Hicks was limping around the mutton kettle, shaking his fist at it and berating it, though in a voice too low for them to hear.

"That's one of your cattle men for you," chuckled Mr. Simms. "I think he would take genuine pleasure in boiling a sheepman in his pot. But he takes the money," added Mr. Simms significantly. "By the way, where's your chum?"

"Whom do you mean?" asked Walter, glancing about the table.

"Chunky, I believe you call him."

"That's so, where is he?" demanded Tad, laying down his fork.

"Probably fallen in somewhere again," growled Ned.

"Did not Master Stacy come in with you, Ned?" asked the Professor hurriedly.

"No, sir."

"He was with you last night?"

"No, not all the time. He went out with me, but I saw him only twice during the early part of my watch."

Mr. Simms looked serious. "I hope nothing has happened to him. See here, Luke. They tell me Master Stacy has not been seen this morning. Know anything of it?"

"Why, no. Are you sure? Have you looked in his tent?"

"Excuse me, I'll go see if he isn't there," said Tad, rising from the table and hurrying to the tent occupied by his companion.

"No," he said as he returned; "evidently he has not been there since we went out at midnight."

"Ask Old Hicks if he has seen him come in," directed Mr. Simms.

The cook said he had not set eyes on the fat boy, adding that he didn't care a rap if he never came back.

The boys looked at each other with mute, questioning eyes.

"We must go in search of him at once," decided the Professor.

"Yes, don't worry, Professor," calmed the rancher. "He has probably strayed off by himself and is unable to find his way back. Luke will round him up in short order. Finish your breakfast, everybody, then we will see that the young man is brought back. Funny he should have gotten away without any one's having noticed it."

"He's always getting himself into trouble," declared Ned.

"I thought I was the only one that did that," retorted Tad, with an attempt at gayety.

"That's different. I know what I'm talking about. Something is sure to happen to that boy before we are ready to go back home."

"Begins to look as if something had already happened," said Walter.

A wild yell startled the sheepmen at the table. It seemed to come from some distance away.

Everybody started up, some reaching for their guns.

"We are attacked!" cried one.

"No, but we're going to be!" shouted another. "There comes one of the boys on a pony giving the alarm."

"Get ready, everybody!"

The camp was in instant confusion. In their haste to prepare for action, the table was upset and its contents piled in a confused heap. Old Hicks was roaring out his displeasure, the foreman was shouting out his orders, while Professor Zepplin was seeking to make himself heard in an effort to give directions to his charges.

Suddenly the voice of the foreman was heard above the uproar.

"Hold on!" he shouted. "It's one of our own - it's --- Oh, bah!"

"What is it? What is it!" cried Mr. Simms, unlimbering his weapon.

"It's Chunky," snorted Ned Rector disgustedly. "The fat boy has been falling in again or I'll eat mutton all the rest of my natural life."

"It sure enough is he," answered Tad, gazing off at the

horseman who was riding at top speed and trying to urge his pony on still faster. "I wonder what he has been getting into this time. Hope it's nothing serious."

"Not to him, anyway, judging by the way he is riding," replied Walter.

"Something has given him a mighty good start, anyhow," shrewdly decided the foreman.

"I know what it is - I know what he's in such a hurry about," said Ned.

"What?" asked Walter.

"Breakfast. He's just found out it's breakfast time," jeered Ned.

"Can't have no breakfast," growled Old Hicks. "Breakfast is et."

"Excepting what's on the ground," added Mary Johnson. "What's he yelling about?"

"Something's gone twisted," decided Champ Blake. "Think so, Noisy?" "Uh-hu," agreed the silent one. All eyes were fixed on Chunky. He was gesticulating wildly and pointing back to the hills from which he had just come.

"I believe they are after us, and in broad daylight, too," snapped Mr. Simms. "Get your ponies. Be quick! Ride fast. Don't let them get near the sheep."

Thus admonished, the sheepmen sprang for their saddles. The boys followed suit at once, leaving only the Professor and Old Hicks to look after the camp.

A bunch of sheep had trotted to a water hole hard by the camp, a faithful shepherd dog following along after them to see that they returned to the main flock as soon as they should have satisfied their thirst. The sheep were now between Chunky and the camp. So intent was he on attracting the attention of the men that he failed to observe the small flock in his path.

Neither did the sheepmen notice it. If Old Hicks did, he did not care what happened either to the sheep or to the boy to whom he had taken such a violent dislike.

"Wow! Wow! Wow!" screamed the boy in a shrill, high-pitched voice.

"What's the matter?"

"Where are they?"

"How many of 'em?"

These and other questions were hurled at Chunky as he dashed straight toward the camp.

He pointed back to the foothills.

"They're there, he says," shouted the foreman. "Come on. Spread out so as to cover the herd. Don't you let a man get through our lines."

Their ponies were stretched out with noses reaching for some unseen object, as it seemed. They swept past the lad within hailing distance, riding hard, while he continued to reach for home.

Stacy had turned to look back at the racing sheepmen, when his pony drove biting and striking right into the flock crowded about the water hole, for the ponies liked the sheep no more than did the cook.

The broncho went down like a flash, hopelessly entangled with the bleating, frightened animals. But Stacy did not stop. That is, he did not do so at once. The lad had shot neatly over the broncho's head, describing a nice curve in the air as he soared.

Pock!

His head landed with a muffled sound.

"Ouch! Help!"

A loud, angry bleat followed his exclamation. The lad's head had been driven with great violence against the soft, unresisting side of a Merino ram.

The Merino went down under the blow. But his soft fleece had saved the boy from serious injury, if not from a broken neck.

"I fell off," cried Stacy, struggling to his feet, running his fingers over his body, as if to determine whether or not he had been hurt. "I - I didn't see them. Th - they got in my way."

Whether he had or not was not now the question, at least so far as the Merino was concerned.

The ram was angry. He resented being bunted over in any such manner.

The animal, scrambling to his feet, uttered a bleat, at the same time viciously throwing up his head, landing lightly, for him, on Chunky's leg.

"Stop kicking me! I say you stop that you -- "

He did not finish what he had started to say. The Merino, finding the mark a satisfactory one, had backed quickly off. With head well down, eyes on the boy who had been the cause of his downfall, he charged with a rush.

Just at the instant when he delivered the blow, the tough, horned head was raised ever so little.

"Ye-o-ow!" shrieked the boy as he felt himself suddenly lifted from his feet and once more propelled through the air head first. It seemed in that brief interval of sailing through space as if every particular bone in his body had been jarred loose from its fastenings. Chunky felt as if he were all falling apart while making his brief second flight.

He was headed straight for the muddy water hole, and the ram was charging him a second time. The lad did not know this, however.

Just at the edge of the water hole the Merino caught him again, neatly flipping him in the air and landing the boy on his back, with a mighty splash, right in the middle of the pool.

Yet the force of the ram's charge had been so great that he was unable to stop when he discovered the water at his feet. In endeavoring to do so, his strong little feet ploughed into the soft turf. The Merino did a pretty half somersault and he too landed in the mud pool on his back.

Unfortunately, he struck in the identical spot that Chunky had, and for a moment there was such a threshing about, such a commotion there as two monsters of the deep might have made in a battle to the death.

Old Hicks was hammering a dishpan on a wheel of the chuck wagon, regardless of the damage he was inflicting on the pan, and screaming with delight.

Professor Zepplin as soon as he could recover his wits, rushed to the rescue and from the flying legs and horns managed to extract Stacy Brown and drag him up to the dry ground.

The lad was a spectacle. Mud was plastered over him from head to foot, while the muddy water was dripping from hair, mouth, ears, eyes and nose.

"I - I fell in, didn't I?" he gasped. "Wh - who kicked me?"

"Who kicked him?" jeered Old Hicks. "Oh, help, help!" he cried, rolling with laughter.

Stacy began to sputter in an uncertain voice.

Professor Zepplin shook him roundly.

"Why didn't you get out of it? The water wasn't over my head, you Chunk," roared Old Hicks.

Chunky eyed him sadly.

"It was the way I went in," he said, breathing hard as he wrung the water from his trousers by twisting them in his hand.

At that the irrepressible Hicks went off into another paroxysm of mirth.

CHAPTER XV

ROPED BY A COWBOY

The Professor had no sooner marched Stacy to his tent to wash the mud from himself and get into a clean suit of clothes, than the sheepmen came galloping back to camp. A few of them had been left out near the foothills in case of a surprise.

"Where's that boy who sent us off on this fool chase?" demanded Luke Larue, riding right into the camp.

Chunky poked his head from the tent, holding the flap about him to cover himself.

"What did you tell us the cowmen were after us for?"

"Who, me?"

"Yes, come out here. I want to talk to you."

"I - I - I can't."

"You'd better or I'll have to fetch you out. Why can't you?" demanded the foreman sternly.

"I - I haven't got any clothes on," stammered the boy.

The foreman slipped from his pony, leaning against a tree with a helpless expression on his face.

Stacy's companions with Mr. Simms and several of the sheepmen rode in at that moment.

"Where's that boy?" demanded the rancher of Larue.

The foreman pointed to the tent. But the lad not yet having finished his toilet, all hands were obliged to stand about waiting for him. They did so with much impatience. Stacy took all the time he needed, apparently not believing that there was any necessity for haste.

At last he sauntered out smiling broadly.

"I think you owe us an explanation, at least," announced Mr. Simms, a peculiar smile playing about the corners of his lips. He had intended to be stern, but the sight of Chunky's good-natured face disarmed him at once, as it did most people.

"'Bout what?" asked the lad.

"Sending us out to the foothills, telling us the cowmen were attacking us."

Stacy's eyes opened widely.

"Never said so."

"What did you say, then?"

"Nothing."

"I guess we are all dreaming," laughed the rancher. "Will you please tell me what did happen then, when you started us away?"

"When I was riding in, you all started up and mounted your ponies. Somebody yelled, 'where are they?' I pointed back to the mountains, and then you rode on," the lad informed him.

It was an unusually long speech for Chunky to make without many halts and pauses. But he did very well with it.

"That is exactly what you did do. When we got there we found not the slightest trace of the cowmen. Where did you see them?"

"I didn't see them," persisted the lad.

"Then why did you tell us you did?"

"I didn't."

Mr. Simms thrust his hands in his pockets and strode back and forth several times.

"Say, young man, did you see anything at all, except what your imagination furnished?"

Chunky nodded emphatically.

"What did you see?"

"Indians."

"Oh, pshaw!" grunted Mr. Simms disgustedly.

"Indians?" interrupted Walter Perkins. "Tell me about it?"

"I was asleep," began Stacy.

"So that's the way you keep watch over our herd is it?" growled Luke. "We were just about to organize a searching party to go after you, when we saw you coming."

"I got tired. I sat down by a rook and - y-a-li - hum -- "

"Ho-ho-ho - hum," yawned the foreman.

Within half a minute the whole outfit was yawning lazily, all save Old Hicks, the cook, who with hands thrust into his trousers pockets stood peering at the fat boy out of the corners of his eyes.

"Stop that, d'ye hear!" snapped Ned Rector angrily. "I'll duck you in that water hole, if you don't."

"Just been ducked," answered Stacy lazily. "Got kicked in by a sheep."

"What about the Indians?" asked Tad impatiently. "I guess you dreamed you saw them."

"No, I didn't. I went to sleep by the rock and when I woke up it was daylight. I yawned."

"Of course you did," jeered Ned. "Wouldn't have been you if you hadn't yawned."

"I was rubbing my eyes and trying to make up my mind where I was when - when -- "

"When what?" urged Tad.

"When somebody said, 'How?'"

The sheepmen laughed.

"I - I looked around, and there - there stood a lot of Indians -- "

"On their heads!" asked Ned.

"No, sitting on their ponies. Then - then I - "

"Then you pitched into them and drove them away," laughed Walter.

"No, I didn't. I yelled and run away. So would you."

Every man and boy of the sheep outfit roared with laughter.

"My boy," said Mr. Simms, "you will have to get used to seeing Indians if you remain with us long. This state is full of them, some bad, some good. But you need not be afraid of them. They dare not interfere with us, so if you see any, just pass the time of day and go on along about your business."

"When I got back here I fell in -- " Professor Zepplin here broke into the conversation to explain what had happened to the fat boy, whereupon the outfit once more shouted with merriment.

The camp finally having been restored to its normal state, plans were made for moving on to the north.

"I wish you would ride over to Groveland Corners and get me fifty feet of quarter inch rope, Tad," said Mr. Simms. "You will have no trouble in finding the way. I'll show you exactly how to get there and find your way back afterwards. And by the way, you might take Philip with you, if you don't mind. I want him to get all the riding he can stand."

"I'll answer yes to both, requests," smiled Tad. "How far is it to the - the -- "

"Corners? Five miles as the crow flies. It will be a slightly longer distance, because you have to go around the Little Butte. The place is situated just behind it on the west side."

"Then, I'm ready now, if Phil is."

The young man was not only ready, but anxious to be off, so without delay, the two lads brought in their ponies and after receiving final instructions as to how to find the new camp, they set off at an easy gallop in the fresh morning air, their spirits rising as they rode over the green mesa that lay sparkling in the morning sunlight.

Groveland Corners was little more than its name implied, consisting of one store that supplied the wants of the half dozen families who inhabited the place, as well as furnishing certain supplies to near-by ranchmen.

A group of cattle men had gathered at the store. They were sitting on the front porch talking earnestly when the two boys rode up. Tad dismounted, hitching his pony, while Phil, shifting to an easy position on his saddle, waited until the purchase of the rope had been made.

The conversation came to a sudden pause as the boys rode up, the cowmen eyeing the newcomers almost suspiciously, Tad thought. However, he paid no attention to them, further than to bid them a pleasant good morning, to which one or two of them gave a grunting reply.

He had noticed one raw-boned mountain boy among the lot who had answered his greeting with a sneering smile and a reply under his breath that Tad had not caught. The lad gave no heed to it, but went about his business. Besides the rope, he made several small purchases for himself. In reply to a question of the storekeeper, Tad informed him that he was with the Simms outfit. One of the cowmen who had entered the store, overhearing this, went outside and informed his companions.

"Hello, kid," greeted one, as the boy left the store. "How's mutton to-day?"

Busily coiling the rope, Tad paid no attention to the taunt; he hung the rope on his saddle horn and then methodically unhitched Pinkeye.

"Going to hang yerself?" jeered another. "That's all a mutton puncher's worth. I guess."

Tad felt his face flush. He paused long enough to turn and look straight into the eyes of the speaker.

"My, but ain't our little boy spunky!" called the fellow in derision.

"If he is, he knows, at least, enough to mind his own business," snapped Tad.

A jeering laugh followed the remark.

"Did ye mean that fer me?" demanded the mountain boy, rising angrily.

"If the coat fits, put it on," answered the freckle-faced boy indifferently, vaulting lightly into the saddle.

"I'll bet that's Boss Simms's kid - the pale-faced dude, eh?" sneered one sharply.

An angry growl answered the suggestion. Tad thinking it was time to be off, turned his pony about and Phil did the same. But no sooner had they headed their mounts toward home, Tad being slightly in the lead, than a rope squirmed through the air.

It dropped over the shoulders of Mr. Simms' delicate young son, tightened about his arms with a jerk.

"Help!" cried the frightened boy.

Tad, glancing back apprehensively saw what had happened. He wheeled his pony like a flash, but not quickly enough to save his companion from falling.

Phil Simms was roped from his pony, landing heavily in the dust of the street.

"Y-e-o-w!" chorused the cowboys.

CHAPTER XVI

TAD WHIPS A MOUNTAIN BOY

Shame! Shame on you!" cried Tad Butler indignantly.

The lad leaped from his pony which he quickly tethered to the hitching bar in front of the store.

This done he ran to his fallen companion, who still lay where the lariat had thrown him. He was half stunned and covered with dust. After jerking him from his pony, however, the cowboys, though continuing their shouts of glee, had made no further effort to molest Philip.

Tad quickly released him.

"I 've had a lot to do with cowboys, but you're the first I ever knew who would do a thing like that. The cowboys I know are gentlemen."

"Then, d'ye mean to say that we ain't, ye miserable cayuse?" demanded one of the number, rising menacingly.

"The fellow who roped that boy is a loafer!" answered Tad bravely, taking a couple of paces forward and facing the crowd. "You wouldn't dare do that to a man,

Frank Gee Patchin

especially if he had a gun as you have. Why didn't you try it on Luke Lame when he was over here?"

"Oh, go back to yer mammy," jeered one.

"I want to know who threw that rope? If he isn't too big a coward, he'll tell me. I guess Mr. Simms will settle with him."

"It's up to you, Bob, I guess," nodded one of them, addressing the angry-faced mountain boy who was one of their number.

The latter rose with what was intended to appear as offended dignity.

"Ye mean me?" he demanded, glaring.

"Yes, if you are the one who did it," answered Tad, looking him squarely in the eyes.

"Then your going to git the alfiredest lickin' you ever had in your life," announced the mountain boy.

Tad held the other with a gaze so steady and unflinching as to cause the mountain boy to pause hesitatingly.

"Phil, jump on your pony and get out of here," directed the lad in a low tone.

"He stays where he is," commanded one of the cowboys.

"Do as I tell you," retorted Tad sharply. "Be quick about it, too."

A cowboy aimed a gun at Phil Simms.

"Try it, if ye want ter git touched up," he warned. "Bob, sail into the fresh kid," he added, nodding his head toward Tad Butler.

"I'm not looking for a fight - I don't want to fight, but if that loafer comes near me I'll have to do the best I can," answered Tad bravely. "I don't expect to get fair play. I'll -- "

"You'll git fair play and you'll git more besides," called the previous speaker. "Go to him, Bob."

Bob lowered his head, sticking out his chin and assuming a belligerent attitude with eyes fixed on the slender figure of his opponent.

Tad was observing the mountain boy keenly, measuring him mentally, while young Simms, pale-faced and frightened, was leaning against his pony, which he had caught and was preparing to mount when he was stopped by the gun of the cowboy.

"See, you've got him rattled already, Bob," shouted a cowman triumphantly. "He'll be running in a minute."

"Come away, Tad," begged Philip.

"Keep quiet. Don't speak to me," answered the lad, without turning his head toward his companion. Tad Butler's whole being was centered on the work that he knew was ahead of him.

He was angry. He felt that he had never been more so in his life, but not a trace of his emotion showed in his face or actions. If he ever had need of coolness, it was at this very moment. He did not know whether he would be able to master the raw-boned mountaineer or not.

The lad's training in athletics had been thorough, and his title of champion wrestler of the high school in Chillicothe had been earned by hard work and persistent effort to make himself physically fit.

"He's all of twenty-five pounds heavier than I am," decided the boy. "I've got to try some tricks that he doesn't know about, if I hope to make any kind of showing."

Bob was now approaching him with an ugly grin on his face. Tad's arms hung easily by his side.

"Come on, what are you waiting for?" Tad smiled.

With a bellow of rage, Bob rushed him.

Tad laughed, and stepping quickly to one side, thrust a foot between the bully's legs as he passed. Bob landed flat on his face in the dust of the street.

The cowboys set up a roar of delight. It was sport, no matter who got the worst of it.

"Give them room," shouted some one, as the men closed quickly about the combatants. "Let the kids fight it out."

These tactics were so new to Bob, that be did not know just what had happened to him. And when he had scrambled to his feet, he met the laughing face of Tad

Butler, which enraged him past all control. This was exactly what Tad wanted.

Bob with a bellow again charged him. Tad made a pass and missed, but covered his failure by neatly ducking under the upraised arm of the cowboy, whose surprised look when he found that he had been punching the empty air brought forth yells of delight from his companions.

Tad had cast away his hat, that it might not interfere with his movements. No sooner had he done so than his opponent renewed his attack. But Tad skillfully parried the heavy blows, delivered awkwardly and without any great amount of skill. The great danger was that his adversary with his superior strength might beat down the lad's defense and land a blow that would put a sudden end to the fray.

Tad was watching for an opening that would enable him to put in practice a plan that had formed in his brain.

"Look out for the cayuse, Bob. He ain't so big a tenderfoot as he looks," warned a cowboy. But Bob had already discovered this fact. Though his fists were beating a tattoo in the air he seemed unable to land a blow on the body of his elusive adversary, and this only served to anger him the more.

"Ki-yi!" yelled the cowboys as a short arm blow, delivered through the mountaineer's windmill movements, reached his jaw and sent him sprawling.

Tad had not been able to put the force into it that he wanted to, else the battle might have ended then and there.

Bob came back. This time he uttered no taunts. The blow hurt him. His head felt dizzy and his fists did not work with the same speed that they had done before.

All at once Tad's right hand shot out, his fist open instead of being closed. It closed over the left wrist of the cowboy with an audible slap.

Tad's left hand joined his right in closing over his adversary's wrist. He whirled sharply, bringing Bob's left arm over his adversary's shoulder. Then something happened that made the cowmen gasp with astonishment. The slender lad lifted the big mountain boy clear of the ground, hurled him over his head, and still clinging to the wrist, brought him down with a smashing jolt, flat on his back in the middle of the village street. Phil Simms narrowly escaped being struck by the heels of the mountain boy's boots as they described a half circle in the air.

Bob lay perfectly still. And for a moment the cowboys stood speechless with amazement.

"Whoopee!" yelled one. "Who-o-o-p-e-e!" chorused the others, dancing about Tad Butler and his fallen victim in wild delight.

"I'm sorry I had to do it," muttered the boy.

They helped Bob to his feet, pounded him on the back, making jeering remarks about his being whipped by a kid, until his courage gradually was urged back as his strength returned.

Suddenly Bob turned on his assailant, and throwing both arms about him, bore him to earth. The move was so unexpected that the lad had no opportunity to side step out of the way. The weight of the mountaineer was so great that Tad found himself unable to squirm from under.

Bob, with a growl of rage, raised his fist, bringing it down with the same movement that he would wield a meat axe.

Tad never flinched as he saw it coming. His eyes were fixed upon the descending fist, his every nerve centered on the task of watching it.

Just at the instant when fist and face seemed to be meeting, the lad by a mighty effort, jerked his head ever so little to the right.

"Oh!" yelled Bob.

Something snapped.

The pressure released from his body, ever so little, Tad by a supreme muscular effort, threw his opponent slightly to one side, and quickly wormed himself from under. He was on his feet in an instant.

The cowboys did not know what had happened, but they knew that the boy from the Simms ranch had done something to their companion that for the instant had taken all of the fight out of him.

Tad had been only partly responsible for Bob's present condition, however. By jerking his head to one side he had caused the mountain boy's fist to strike the hard roadbed instead of Tad's head.

Bob struggled to his feet, holding the right wrist with the left hand and moaning with pain. The right hung limp. Tad knew what had happened.

"He's broken his wrist. I'm glad I didn't have to do it for him," said the lad.

At first glowering glances were cast in Tad's direction. They were of half a mind to punish him in their own way.

"You said it was to be a fair fight," spoke up the lad. "Has it been?"

There was a momentary silence.

"The kid's right," exclaimed a cowman. "He cleaned up Bob fair and square. I reckon you kin go, now."

"Thank you."

"Hold on a minute. Not so fast, young fellow. I'm kinder curious like to know how ye put Bob over yer head like that!" asked another.

"It was a simple little Japanese wrestling trick," laughed the boy.

"Kin ye do that to me?"

"I don't know."

"Well, yer going ter try and right here and now."

"All right, come over here on the grass where the ground isn't so hard. If I succeed in doing it, though, you must agree not to get mad. I can't fight you, you know. You are too big for me."

The cowman grinned significantly, and strode over to the place indicated by Tad Butler.

"Now what d'ye want me ter do?" he demanded, leering. "Yer see I'm willing?"

"Strike at me, if you wish. I don't care how you go about it," replied Tad.

"Here goes!"

The cowman launched a terrific blow with his right. Tad sprang back laughing.

"If that had ever hit me, you never would have known how the other trick is worked," he said, while the cowboys laughed uproariously at the fellow's surprise when he found that his fist had not landed.

"Guess the kid ain't no slouch, eh, Jim?" jeered one.

Jim let go another, then a third one. The third blow proved his undoing. The next instant Jim's boots were describing a half circle in the air over Tad Butler's head. His revolvers slipping from their holsters in transit, dropped to the ground and Jim landed flat on his back with a mighty grunt.

He was up with a roar, his right hand dropping instinctively to his empty holster.

"Wh-o-o-o-e!" warned the fellow's companions. "No fair, Jim. No fair. He said as he'd do it, and he did. Kid, you'd clean out the whole outfit, give you time, I reckon."

Jim pulled himself together, restored his weapons to their places, and walked over to Tad, extending his hand.

"That was a dizzy wallop ye give me, pardner," he. said, with a sheepish grin. "If ye'll show me how it's did, I'll call it square."

Tad laughingly did so.

"I guess I couldn't get even with them any easier than by showing them the trick," he grinned, mounting his pony, and accompanied by Philip rode away. "They'll try that trick till the whole bunch of them get into a battle royal."

They did, as Tad learned next day.

CHAPTER XVII

CHUNKY RIDES THE GOAT

"There's the sheep," announced Tad, after they had ridden on for some time.

"I'm glad," said Phil, "do you know, Tad, I thought those men were going to kill you." Phil's courage had returned, when he realized that they were in sight of friends once more.

Tad laughed.

"They aren't half so bad as they would have us believe. The boy was the worst of the lot. He needed to he taught a lesson, but I wish I hadn't hurt him," he mused.

"He did it himself; you didn't."

"Yes, I know. I had to to save my own face." The lad laughed heartily at his own joke, which Philip, however, failed to catch. "Now we'll find out where the camp is," said Tad, espying a herder off to the north of them.

Having been directed to the new camp, Phil galloped away, Tad remaining to chat with the sheepman a few minutes. Yet he made no mention of his experience at Groveland Corners, not being particularly proud of it, after all. After riding slowly about with, the herder for half an hour, the lad jogged off toward camp, which his companion had reached before him.

Philip had spread the story of Tad's battle with the cowboy. Old Hicks, contrary to his usual practice, had listened with one ear, giving a grunt of satisfaction when the story had been told. As a result there were several persons eagerly awaiting him in the sheep camp when he rode up.

"Who's getting into trouble now?" demanded Stacy, with mock seriousness. "You need a guardian, I guess. I presume Mr. Simms thinks so, too."

"Heard you had two black eyes," jeered Ned Rector.

"Say, Tad, we've agreed that you shall show us how you did it, using Chunky for your model," said Walter Perkins.

Tad smiled good-naturedly, dismounting from the saddle and tethering the pony with his usual care.

"Guess I'd better leave the saddle on. There may he something doing any minute," he mused.

"Mr. Simms wants ye over to his tent," Old Hicks informed Tad.

"Oh, all right," answered the lad, walking briskly to the little tent occupied by the owner of the herd.

The foreman was there awaiting Tad's arrival as well.

"First I want to thank you for having taken Phil's part so splendidly," glowed Mr. Simms. "It is a wonder they did not do you some harm after that."

"Oh, they were not half bad," laughed Tad. "They were ashamed of what they'd done after it was all over."

"No. There's no shame in that crowd. I know them. Phil has told me about it. I know them all, and they shall suffer for roping that boy," went on the rancher angrily.

"One of them has," answered Tad, with a mischievous twinkle in his eyes. "Besides, there's going to be a big fight over there. Perhaps they are at it now."

"Fight? I should judge from what I hear that there already has been one. What do you mean?"

"Oh, nothing very serious. I taught them the Japanese trick of throwing a man over my head. They were trying it on when I left. Shouldn't be surprised, after they learn how to do the trick, if they got mad and had a real fight."

Luke Larue leaned back, slapping his thighs and laughing uproariously.

"Well, you are a smart one," he exclaimed. "Couldn't lick them all yourself, so you fixed it so they'd sail in and lick each other. Funniest thing I ever heard. I'll have to tell Old Hicks about that. But I won't do it till after dinner, or he'll burn the mutton and spoil our meal. Fighting each other!" Luke indulged in more hilarity.

"You heard nothing, of course - they said nothing about our herd -- "

"No, but it was plain that they had no love for you, Mr. Simms. It was the boy who roped Philip, though. I do not think the men would have done anything like that."

"It's all the same. It shows the feeling that exists. Nothing will ever wipe that out except a good whipping. It's coming to them and they are going to get it."

"You think then - you believe they have not given up their plan of attacking the sheep?" asked Tad.

"Given it up? Not they. They have been too well nagged on by your friend of the Rosebud. I wish I knew who he is. I probably never shall, though."

"I'll know him if I see him again."

"You might not. Camp-fire sight is tricky."

"I'll know his voice, sir. I presume you will continue your watch over the herd to-night?"

"Yes, and for many nights to come. We shall keep it up until we get far enough to the north so that we are sure there will be no trouble. I guess you had better go on the late trick to-night. That is the most important. We'll send your friend Chunky out early in the evening. His habit of going to sleep at unusual times is too serious to trust him with the late and dangerous watch. If they strike it will be close to morning, I imagine."

"I hope they won't, for your sake."

"So do I," answered Mr. Simms, with emphasis.

The afternoon was waning. The Pony Riders were all in camp, some reading, others writing letters home, for already much had happened that would make interesting reading to the folks off in the little Missouri town.

Steam was rising from the big kettle, into which Old Hicks was about to drop a quarter of mutton for the evening meal, and an air of perfect peace hovered over the camp of the sheepmen. Under a spreading tree the bell goat of the outfit lay stretched out sound asleep. He had been in that position most of the afternoon, there being nothing special for him to do, as the herd was grazing as it saw fit, without any effort being made to urge it along.

From the other side of the tree the round face of Stacy Brown might have been observed peering to one side of the sleeping goat.

He listened intently. Billy was breathing short, regular breaths, with no thought of the trouble that was in store for him. From the expression of the boy's face it was evident that he was forming some mischievous plan of his own. This was verified when, after dodging back behind the tree, his head appeared once more and a stick was cautiously thrust out. Slowly it was pushed toward Billy's nose, which it gently rubbed and then was withdrawn.

Billy probably thought it was a fly, for one impatient hoof brushed the troubled nose; then the interrupted nap was continued.

Stacy tried it again with equal success. His sides were shaking with laughter, and every little while he would hide himself behind the tree to give vent to his merriment.

The others were too busy to notice what he was doing, though once Old Hicks paused in his work to cast a suspicious glance in that direction.

Stacy had been amusing himself for several minutes and with such success that he grew more bold. He had stepped from behind the tree that he might the better reach his victim. Now the tickling and the sweep of the impatient hoof became more frequent. Billy grunted as if he were having a bad dream, and this amused Stacy so much that he was obliged to retire behind the tree again to laugh.

As he emerged this time, Billy slowly opened a cautious eye, all unobserved by his tormentor. With a hand over his own mouth to keep back the laughter, the lad rubbed the stick gently over the goat's nose. Billy's chin whiskers took an almost imperceptible upward tilt and the observing eye opened a little more widely.

Next time Stacy varied the performance by giving the goat a malicious little dig in the ribs with the sharp end of the stick.

Billy rose up into the air as if hurled there by an explosion beneath him. When he landed on his four feet, it was with head pointed directly toward the foe and with fore legs sloping well back under him ready for a drive with his tough little head.

"Oh!" exclaimed Chunky, rapping the goat smartly

over the nose with the stick to drive the animal off.

Billy drove all right, but it was not away from the lad. Stacy was standing with legs apart and Billy dived between them, at the same time lifting his head.

The effect was instantaneous. Chunky was neatly flipped to the goat's back, face down with his legs dangling about the animal's neck. Instinctively he took a quick grip with the legs, locking his feet on the underside of Billy's neck and his hands about the withers.

At that moment the surprised goat gave an excellent imitation of a broncho trying to throw its rider.

"Hel-p!" cried Chunky in a muffled voice.

No one save the cook heard it.

"Whoop!" bellowed Old Hicks, smiting his thigh with a mighty fist and screaming with laughter.

The Pony Riders and everyone else in camp sprang to their feet, not understanding what the commotion was about.

"The kid's riding the goat," yelled Hicks. "He's initiating himself into the order of Know Nuthins. See him buck! See him buck!"

The camp roared.

"Let go, Chunky!" shouted Walter.

"I can't, I'll fall off," answered the boy in a scarcely

audible voice.

"I'll help you then. Come on, boys."

They made a concerted rush to rescue their companion. This was the signal for the goat to adopt new tactics. He probably thought it was some new form of torture that they had planned for him.

Billy headed for the tent of the owner of the herd. He went through it like a projectile, upsetting the folding table on which Mr. Simms was writing, and out through the flap at the other end.

By this time the outfit was in an uproar. Even the sheep on the range near by paused in their grazing to gaze curiously campward; the herders off in that direction shaded their eyes against the sun and tried to make out the cause of the disturbance.

"Y-e-o-w!" encouraged the cook, waving a loaf of bread above his head and dancing about with a more pronounced limp than usual.

Jerk, jerk, went Chunky's head until he feared it would be jerked from his body.

"Stay by him, stay by him, kid," encouraged a sheepman.

Mr. Simms rushing from his tent, startled and angry, instantly forgot the words of protest that were on his lips and joined heartily in laughter at the ludicrous sight.

"Look out that you don't lose your stirrups," jeered

Ned as goat and rider shot by him with a bleat.

Walter made a grab for Billy with the result that he was pivoting on his own head the next second.

Once they thought Chunky was going to fall off and put a sudden end to their fun, but he soon righted himself, whereupon he tightened the grip of hands and legs.

By this time the goat was mad all through. He seemed bent now upon doing all the damage he could.

"Stop that! Want to run me down!" shouted Ned, grabbing a tree as the outfit swept by him, the goat uttering a sharp bleat and Chunky a howl of protest.

All at once Billy headed for the kitchen department. Old Hicks saw him coming and with a few quick hops got out of the way.

"Hi there, hang you, where you heading?" he roared.

The tinware had been stacked up on a bench to dry out in the sunlight. Perhaps it was the rays of the sun on the bright tin that attracted Billy's attention. At any rate he went through it with a bound, amid the crash of rattling tin and splintering wood.

Old Hicks made a swing at the animal with the long stick he had been using to prod the kettle of mutton. He missed and sat down suddenly, his lame leg refusing to bear the strain that had been put upon it.

It was astonishing the endurance the goat showed, for Chunky was no light weight in any sense of the word.

Now and then he would just graze the trunk of a tree, bringing a howl from his rider as the latter's leg was scraped its full length against the bark of the tree.

By this time nearly everyone in camp had laughingly sought places of safety, some in the chuck wagon, others climbing saplings as best they could, for no man knew in what direction Billy might head next.

Old Hicks refused to take the protection that the wagon offered. He stood his ground, stick held firmly in both hands, awaiting a chance to rap the boy or the goat when they next passed.

His opportunity came soon. He had been baking pies for the sheepmen's supper and these he had placed on the tail board of the wagon, which he had removed and laid upon a frame made of sticks stuck into the ground.

Billy finished the pies in one grand charge.

The enraged cook forgot his own danger and boldly striding out into the open began throwing things at the mad goat. It mattered not what he threw. Anything he laid his hands on answered for the purpose - dishpans, small kettles, knives, loaves of bread - all went the same way, some of them reaching Chunky and bringing a howl from him. The goat, however, escaped without being hit once.

Twice more after wrecking the pies, did he charge the kitchen. It was noticed, however, that he avoided the hot stove. Hicks gladly would have lost that for the sake of seeing the goat smash against it and end his career.

After one drive more ferocious than any he had made before, Billy whirled and came back. Old Hicks stood with his back to the kettle, stick held aloft. He was going to get the goat this time, for he saw the animal would pass close to him if he held his present course.

Billy did so until within a few feet of the cook. Then he changed his direction. He changed it more suddenly than the cook had looked for.

Billy's head hit Old Hicks a powerful blow. The cook doubled up with a grunt. When he came down he landed fairly in the kettle of hot mutton. Cook and kettle toppled over, the former yelling for help and struggling desperately to extricate himself.

Chunky too had fared badly in the final charge. The shock had thrown him sideways and he crumpled up not far from the kettle and its human occupant.

They fished Old Hicks from the wreck, fuming and raging and threatening to kill the goat and to chase the "heathen kid" out of the camp.

Chunky was limp and breathless when they picked him up. They dragged the lad away from the vicinity of the cook as quickly as possible. Old Hicks' rage at that moment was a thing to avoid. The goat, Billy, galloped away, the least disturbed of the outfit, but it was observed that he prudently remained out on the range with the sheep that night.

"I didn't fall in that time, did I?" gasped Chunky, after his breath had come back sufficiently to enable him to talk.

"No, but you're going to do so when the cook gets hold of you," warned Ned.

"Hicks? Old Hicks fell into the mutton broth, didn't he?" chuckled the fat boy.

CHAPTER XVIII

THE VIGIL BY THE FOOTHILLS

Supper was late in the sheep camp that evening. Old Hicks was in a terrible rage and no one dared protest at the delay, for fear he would get no supper at all. The boys were still discussing Stacy Brown's feat, and every time the subject was referred to all during the evening, it was sure to elicit a roar of laughter.

As night came on, the sky was gradually blotted out by a thin veil of clouds, which seemed to grow more dense as the evening wore on. Chunky had been sent out with Mary Johnson on guard duty, Walter having gone out with the foreman. That left Tad Butler and Ned Rector of the Pony Rider Boys, to take their turn on the late trick.

Tad preferred to sit up rather than to try to sleep for the short time that would intervene before it came his turn to go out.

"Do you think we shall have any trouble tonight?" he asked, looking up as Mr. Simms passed his tent.

"You know as much about that as I do, my boy. Perhaps your courage over at the Corners may scare them off, eh? They may think, if we are all such fighters over here, that it will be a good place to keep away from."

Tad laughed good-naturedly.

"Guess I didn't give them any such fright as that. How is Philip this evening?"

"Sound asleep. It's doing the boy good. He hasn't slept like this since his illness last spring."

"I wish he might go on with us and spend the summer out of doors."

"H-m-m-m," mused Mr. Simms. "I am afraid he would be too great a care. No, Tad, the boy is a little too young. Where are you going next?"

"I am not sure."

"Well, let me know when you find out and we will talk it over. Fine night for a raid of any kind, isn't it?"

"Yes, sir," answered Tad, glancing up at the black clouds.

"Good luck to you to-night. You and your partner must take care of yourselves. Do not take any unnecessary risk. You will have done your part in using your keen young eyes to see that no one gets near the camp."

"I should feel better if I had a gun," laughed the boy. "Somehow - but no, I guess it is not best."

"Certainly not."

Tad turned up the lantern in his tent and sat down to his book, which he had been reading most of the evening. He was not interrupted again until the camp watchmen came around to turn out the second guard.

Ned was asleep and he tumbled out rubbing his eyes, not sure just what was wanted of him.

"Wake up," laughed Tad. "You are getting to be a regular sleepy head."

"Guess I am. Is - is it time to go out?"

"It is. And it is a dark night, too."

"Whew! I should say it is," replied Ned, with an apprehensive glance out beyond the camp. "How are we ever going to find our way about to-night?"

"I don't imagine we shall be moving about much after we get on our station. Mr. Larue will place us there."

"Where are we going to be?"

"He hasn't said. I did hear him say that we were going to watch singly instead of in pairs, in order that he might cover more territory with the men at his disposal."

"Sounds shivery."

"I don't know why it should. It is night, that is the only difference. I am getting used to being out in the night and not knowing where I am," laughed Tad.

Tucking the lunches that had been wrapped for them

into their pockets, the two boys walked over to the place where their ponies were tethered. The animals had been left bridled and saddled, the saddle girths having been loosened. These the boys tightened and prepared to mount when Tad happened to think of something.

"Hold my pony, Ned. I want to get something from the tent."

Tad returned a moment later with his lariat, which he coiled carefully and hung to the saddle horn, Ned Rector observing him with an amused smile.

"If you can't shoot them you're going to rope them, eh?"

"A rope is always a good thing to have with you. You don't think so, but it is. Never know what minute you are going to need it badly."

"It wouldn't do me any good, no matter how much I needed it," smiled Ned. "I couldn't lasso the side of a barn."

"You do very well. If you will practise every day you will be able to handle it as well as the average cowboy in less than a week. Come along."

As they left the camp, Luke Larue met them to conduct the boys to the places where they were to spend the last half of the night.

"After we leave the herd behind us, it's the frozen tongue for you," he said.

"You mean we are not to speak?" asked Tad.

"Not a word out loud. If you have anything you must say, whisper."

"Oh, all right."

They dropped Ned first. His station was nearer to the herd than that which had been assigned to Tad. The latter went on with the foreman until they were fairly out by the foothills.

"I've given you one of the most responsible stations, you see," whispered the foreman. "It will be lonesome out here. Do you mind?"

"Not at all. Anybody near me?"

"Noisy Cooper is over there to your left about ten rods away. Bat Coyne is to your right here. You're not so close that you can rub elbows, however. Be watchful. It's just the night for a raid. Use your own judgment in case you hear anything suspicious. Above all look out for yourself. You've got a pony that will take you away from trouble pretty fast if you get in a hurry. You know the signal?"

"Yes."

"Then good night and good luck," whispered Luke, reaching out and giving Tad's hand a hearty clasp.

There was something so encouraging - so confident in the grip, that even had Tad Butler's courage been waning, it would have come back to him with a rush after that.

"Good night," he breathed. "I'll be on the spot if anything occurs."

"I know that," answered the foreman. In an instant Luke had been swallowed up in the great shadow and not even the hoof beats of his pony were audible to the listening ears of the boy.

Tad looked about him inquiringly. As his eyes became more used to the darkness he found himself able to make out objects about him, though the darkness distorted them into strange shapes.

"I think I'll get under that tree," he decided. "No one can see me there. They'd pick me out here in a minute. The cowboys have eyes as well as ears. I know that, for I've lived with them."

The lad tightened on the reins ever so little, and the pony pricking up its ears moved away with scarcely a sound, as if realizing that extreme caution were expected of it.

They pulled up under the shadow of the tree. There, Tad found that he could see what lay about him even better than before.

He patted Pink-eye on the neck and a swish of the animal's tail told him that the little attention was appreciated.

"Good boy," soothed the lad, running his fingers through the mane, straightening out a kink here and there.

He had dropped the reins as he finished with the mane,

and Pink-eye's head began to droop until his nose was almost on the ground. He had settled himself for the long vigil. Perhaps he would go to sleep in a few moments. The rider hoped he would, for then there would be no movement that a stranger might hear.

It was a lonesome post. There was scarcely a sound, though now and then a bird twittered somewhere in the foliage and once he beard the mournful hoot of an owl far away to his left.

"I wonder if that could have been a signal, or was it a real bird," whispered Tad to himself. "I have heard of a certain band of outlaws that always used the hoot of the owl as their signal to each other."

After an interval of perhaps a minute another owl wailed out its weird cry off to his right.

Tad Butler pricked up his ears.

"Well, if it isn't a signal, those owls are holding a regular wireless conversation. Hark!"

Far back in the foothills there sounded another similar call.

Tad Butler was sure, by this time, that something was going on that would bear watching.

For a long time he heard nothing more, and was beginning to think that perhaps he had drawn on his imagination too far. It might be owls after all.

"I wonder if the others heard that, too? Maybe they know better than I what it means, if it means anything at all. I wish Mr. Larue would happen along now. I'd like to tell him what I think."

He knew, however, that the foreman, like himself was stationed somewhere off there in the blackness, sitting on his pony as immovable as a statue, his straining eyes peering into the night, his ears keyed to catch the slightest sound.

A gentle breeze rippled over the trees, stirring the foliage into a soft murmur. Then the breeze passed on and silence once more settled over the scene.

Tad sighed. Even a little wind was a welcome break in the monotony. He was not afraid, but his nerves were on edge by this time, and Tad made no attempt to deny it.

Something snapped to the left of him. The sound was as if some one had stepped on a dry branch which had crumpled under his weight.

The lad was all attention instantly.

"There certainly is something over there," he whispered. "It may be a man, but I'll bet it's a bear or some other animal. If it's a bear, first thing I know Pink-eye will bolt and then I'll be in a fix."

Tad cautiously gathered up the reins, using care not to disturb the pony, for it was all important that the animal remain absolutely quiet just now.

But, though the boy listened with straining ears, there was no repetition of the sound and this led him to believe that it had been an animal, which perhaps had scented them and was stalking him already.

It was not a comforting thought. Yet Tad never moved. He sat in his saddle rigidly, every nerve and muscle tense. He was determined to be calm no matter what happened.

The lad's head was thrown slightly forward, his chin protruding stubbornly, and as he listened there was borne to his ears another sound. It was as if something was approaching with a soft tread. He could hear it distinctly.

"Whatever that thing is, it has four feet," decided the lad quickly. "It's not a man, that is sure."

Instinctively he permitted his left hand to drop to the pommel of the saddle so that he might not be unseated in case Pink-eye should take sudden alarm and leap to one side. The reins were lightly bunched in the left, Tad's right hanging idly at his side.

The footsteps became more and more pronounced, Tad's curiosity increasing in proportion.

He fully expected to see a bear lumber from the shadows at any second now. If this happened he did not know what he should do. Of course he could ride away, but in doing so he might alarm the watching sheepmen and upset all their plans.

The noise after approaching for some moments, suddenly ceased. Tad's eyes were fairly boring into the shadows. All at once the particular shadow at which he was looking moved.

Tad started violently.

The shadow moved forward a few steps, then halted.

It was a man on horseback. He had ridden right out from the foothills.

"It's here," whispered Tad Butler to himself. The rider moved up a few steps again, this time halting within a few feet of the watching boy.

Tad's hand cautiously stole down to his lariat. He brought it up at arm's length, held it for one brief moment then swung it over his head.

CHAPTER XIX

A CLEVER CAPTURE

His plan had been conceived in a flash and executed almost as quickly.

The rawhide rope squirmed through the air. He could not be sure of his aim in the darkness, but the stranger was so close that Tad did not believe he could miss. He knew that if he did, he would find himself in a serious predicament.

He heard a sudden startled exclamation.

At that instant, Pink-eye, alarmed by the unusual movement on his back, awakened and leaped lightly to one side.

"I've got him," breathed the boy, feeling the line draw tight under his hand. "I've caught a man I -- "

Pink-eye had discovered the presence of strangers now and with a snort he changed his position by again leaping to one side. Tad heard the man strike the ground with a grunt. He took a turn of the lariat around the saddle pommel, drawing it taut.

"Who are you!" demanded the lad.

Frank Gee Patchin

A snarl of rage and a struggle over there on the ground was his only answer.

"Get up, if you don't want to be dragged. If you make a loud noise it will be the worse for you," announced the boy sternly.

He clucked to the pony, which started forward suddenly, throwing a strain upon the rope.

"Steady, Pink-eye. We don't want to hurt him," he cautioned, slowing the animal down to almost a walk.

"Are you on your feet back there?"

"Y-y-y-yes."

There came a sharp jerk on the line. The boy knew that the man he had roped, pinioning his arms to his side had managed to get his hands up and grasped the line. In a moment he would free himself.

Tad pressed the rowels of his spurs against Pink-eye's sides. The animal sprang forward, but the boy quickly checked him, pulling him down into a jog trot that was not beyond the endurance of a man to follow for a short distance.

"Remember if you allow yourself to fall down I'll drag you the rest of the way in," warned Tad Butler. "I won't hurt you if you behave yourself."

"Le - le - let me go. I - I - I - I - aint't done n-n-nothing."

"We'll decide that when I get you back to camp,"

answered Tad. "And don't let me hear you raising your voice again or I'll put spurs to the pony. Do you understand?"

"Y-y-y-e-s."

On the soft ground the footfalls of the pony made no sound that could be heard any distance away. On ahead of him the lad saw the dim light of a lantern, which he knew was at the camp and his heart leaped exultantly at the thought of what he had accomplished. He wondered if the others or any of them had done as well.

"Won't Mr. Simms be surprised?" he glowed.

"Wait, I - I - I'm going to drop," came a voice from behind him. It sounded far away and indistinct.

"You'd better not unless you want to go the rest of the way lying on your back," called back the lad. However, he slackened the speed of his pony a little, thinking that perhaps his prisoner might be in distress. Tad was too tender hearted to cause another to suffer, even if it were an enemy.

The lad kept his left hand on the rope. In this way he was able to judge how well the man was following. Now and then a violent jerk told Tad that he was experimenting to see if he could not get away. The fellow might have braced his feet and possibly snapped the line, but he evidently feared to do this lest he be thrown on his face and dragged that way, for the noose of the lariat had, by this time, so tightened about his body as to bind his arms tightly to his side.

Tad uttered a warning whistle.

Instantly he noted figures moving about the camp. His call had been heard. The camp-fire was stirred to give more light, and as its embers flared up, Tad Butler and his prisoner galloped in.

At first they did not observe that he had a man in tow.

Old Hicks hobbled forward with a growl and a demand to know what the row was about.

"What is it, boy? What is it? Are they coming!" exclaimed Mr. Simms, running toward him.

"I've got a man. I can't stop. Grab him!" cried Tad in an excited, triumphant tone.

Mr. Simms saw. The others observed at the same time. They made a concerted rush for the lad's prisoner.

"Stop!" commanded the rancher.

Tad drew up instantly. As he did so three of them grabbed the man at the other end of the lariat, throwing him on the ground flat on his back.

"All right?" sang back Tad.

"Yes."

The boy unwound the rope from his saddle pommel and casting the end from him, rode back and dismounted. Yes, he had caught a cowman, but the fellow sullenly refused to answer a question that was put to him.

The prisoner was glaring up at him with eyes so full of malignant hate that Tad instinctively shrank back.

"Know him!" asked Mr. Simms sharply.

"Not by name. He's one of the men I saw over at the Corners. He was the worst one of the lot, except the boy they called Bob."

No amount of questioning, however, would draw the fellow out. They had bound him hand and foot and straightened up to view their work.

"There's no use in wasting time," decided Mr. Simms. "Drag him over to my tent and throw him in. Did you hear anybody besides this man"

Tad told him about the owl calls. The rancher pondered a few seconds.

"That sounds to me more like an Indian trick. But I am satisfied we are going to be attacked tonight. You had better go back to your post. Can you find the way?"

"Yes, I think so," answered the lad.

"Boy, you've done a great piece of work. I'll talk with you about it when we have more time. I must hurry out and find Luke. The rest of you stick by the camp until you know that the cowmen are here; then sail in. There'll likely be some shooting."

"Any further instructions?" asked Tad, bunching the reins in his hand preparatory to mounting.

"Nothing. That is, unless you find you can rope some

more of these cayuses. I'd like to have them all tied up here for a while. I've got a few things to say to them. They'd have to listen whether they wanted to or not if they were all in the same fix that fellow is," he added with a short, mirthless laugh.

Tad swung himself into the saddle, first having coiled his rope and hung it in its place.

"Good-bye," he sang out, starting out at a gallop and disappearing in the night.

As Tad drew near the scene of his recent experience, he slowed the pony down to a walk, moving on with extreme caution. He did not want to fall into the trap that the cowboy had only a short time before.

After groping about in the darkness some time, he finally came upon the very tree that had sheltered him before.

Tad uttered a low exclamation of satisfaction, once more taking up his position under its spreading branches. He had been there but a short time when the foreman rode up, giving a low whistle so that the boy would know who it was.

"Anything develop?"

"Yes."

"What?"

Tad told him briefly of the capture of the cowboy.

"Good boy," glowed Luke, reaching over and slapping

Tad on the back approvingly. "I guess we made no mistake in giving you this post. But there's not likely to be any more of them come through this way. I am going to send you down nearer the center. We are going to have all the fun we want before morning. So I wish you would move down nearer the herd. When the racket begins, if it does, we shall need all the sheepmen to help drive off the raiders. You will relieve one of them and look after the sheep. I have told your friend Ned the same thing. He's down there now."

"Where are the sheep?"

"Head just a little to your left and ride straight, on till you come up with them. But be sure to give the whistle now and then so our men will know who you are if they chance to hear you coming. Did anybody know the fellow you roped?"

"No. I saw him at the store yesterday, though."

"Guess you've made no mistake then. Well, so long."

Tad missed his way in the darkness, and had roamed about for some time before finally coming up with the herd. Even then he was at a part of the line where there seemed to he no one on guard.

He whistled and waited. After a little the signal was answered It was then only a matter of a few moments before he had joined the herder and delivered his message.

The man rode away to take up his new position and Tad settled down to tending sheep. There was little for him to do, the animals being sound asleep, but he

Frank Gee Patchin

rather enjoyed the relief from the strain that he had been under while watching for intruders off yonder under the tree.

Dismounting, the boy sat down on the ground, having stripped the reins over the pony's neck so that he could keep them in his hand. Pinkeye nibbled at the grass a few seconds. It did not seem to satisfy the animal, for the sheep had worked it pretty well down ahead of him. So Pink-eye went to sleep, and Tad found himself nodding so persistently that he forced himself to get up and walk back and forth a few paces each way.

"I am getting to be as much of a sleepy head as Chunky is," he smiled. "That goat ride was the funniest thing I ever saw. I wonder where Billy took himself to. He's a wise goat. I actually believe he had more fun out of putting the camp to the bad than the rest of us experienced in watching him."

Pink-eye woke up and rubbed his nose against the boy's coat sleeve.

A shrill whistle trilled out off to the west. It was followed by another and another, until the air seemed full of them.

Tad paused abruptly in his walk and listened.

A pistol spat viciously. He caught the flash faintly in the distance.

Tad threw the reins over Pink-eye's neck and vaulted into the saddle. Boy and pony were both wide awake now.

CHAPTER XX

THRILLING RESCUE OF THE RANCHER

They're here," breathed the lad. "I wonder what's going to happen."

As if in answer to his question, a volley of pistol shots sounded to the west of him. Almost instantly following, guns began to pop to the north and south.

Shouts and yells sounded everywhere.

Startled, half a hundred sheep near him, scrambled to their feet.

"W-h-o-e-e-e," soothed Tad, turning toward them as he remembered that he had a duty to perform. "Come now, Pink-eye, never mind the shooting. Just you and I attend to our business. That's what we've got to do."

Yet Tad regretted that he was not over there in the thick of the fight. He gave a long whistle, hoping to find some one near him. The whistle was not answered, therefore he concluded that he was alone on that side of the herd. But where was Ned? He should be somewhere near by.

By this time the restless herd required his whole

Frank Gee Patchin

attention. Tad galloped up and down the line, speaking soothing words to the frightened sheep, whistling and trying to sing.

"Here, Barker," he cried, discovering that he was not alone in his efforts. One of the sheep dogs was trotting along by his side, uttering little encouraging yelps to assist in keeping the lines well formed. "That's a good dog. I guess you and I can handle this outfit, can't we, Barker?"

Barker barked as if in approval of the sentiment.

Tad called the animal to him and sent him back the other way, while he pressed on. The noise of the conflict seemed to be up that way and it was at that end that there would be more likelihood of disturbance to the sheep, he thought, urging his pony along a little faster.

All at once guns began to flash ahead of him.

"I believe they are in the flock already," he cried, putting spurs to Pink-eye and dashing on at top speed. "Yes, they are shooting into the flock. I can tell by the flashes of their guns. Oh, if I had a gun!"

The thought that they were slaughtering the innocent animals roused all the fighting blood in Tad Butler's nature.

But what could he, single-handed and unarmed, expect to do to stop the ruthless slaughter?

From the opposite direction, he heard a body of horsemen bearing down on the sheep killers.

In a moment more they too began to shoot. He noted quickly, however, that this latter body of men were not shooting down. They were shooting over the heads of the herd at the men who were killing the stock.

"Good! Good! Give it to them!" fairly screamed the lad, rising in his stirrups, waving his hat and continuing his words of encouragement to the men of Mr. Simms's outfit. What mattered it whether they could hear him or not? A rattling fire was running along both lines of men. But the sheep killers, now content to ride down the sheep, were shooting back at their assailants.

"Somebody will be killed, I know," cried Tad. "Who's there?" he roared, as he heard the hoof beats of a running pony behind him.

"It's me, Chunky," came the answer.

"Get out of here, boy. You will be killed."

"I can't. I'm afraid to stay back there in the camp all alone. Hicks has gone too and -- "

"Then get back down the line and help me to hold these sheep. Don't give anyone a chance to say a Pony Rider Boy is afraid of anything. How'd you like to be over there where those guns are going off? Now, brace up. Look cheerful and tend to those sheep the same as Barker is doing."

Thus admonished, Stacy did brace up.

"All right," he said, pulling himself together and turning his pony about.

In the meantime the shouting had increased in volume and the shooting was more rapid. Tad had all he could do to hold the sheep in place. He knew that up above him they were rushing wildly here and there, and the wave of terror rolled over those in his immediate vicinity.

"They're beating them back!" cried the boy. "The cowboys are giving way. Hooray!"

This proved to be the case. The defense of the sheepmen was a surprise to the cowboys, where they had thought to surprise the sheep herders and stampede the herd before any opposition was offered.

With a yell of triumph the forces under Mr. Simms rode right over the scurrying sheep in their effort to drive the cowmen off.

At that moment the clouds parted and the full moon shone out, lighting up the scene brightly. Tad gazed in awe on the rushing ponies as he pulled his own to a stop. The cowmen, too, seemed to take courage from the moonlight. Some had started to retreat. These whirled about and returned to the charge.

"Oh, there goes Mr. Simms!" cried the boy.

He saw the rancher waver in the saddle, throw up his hands and slip sideways with head and arms hanging down.

"He's shot! He's shot! They don't see him!" shouted Tad. He cried out at the top of his voice to attract the attention of the ranchers, but in the uproar, no one heard him. His voice in that mad melee was a puny thing.

Fortunately the rancher's feet still clung to the stirrups, but his head was hanging so low that it appeared to be bumping along the ground with every leap of his pony, which was headed straight for the lines of the enemy.

"Oh, why won't they see him!" groaned the lad. "I can't stand it to sit here doing nothing and see a man lose his life that way - if he's not dead already."

Tad, acting upon a sudden resolve, shook out his reins, gave the pony a quick pressure with the spurs.

"Hi-yi!" he snapped.

Pink-eye leaped forward, with Tad urging him to renewed efforts by sharp slaps on the animal's thigh. The boy was not shouting now. He did not wish to attract attention to himself if it could be avoided. In order to head off the rancher's pony, Tad was compelled to follow an oblique direction which, if he continued it, would land him fairly in the center of the enemy's lines.

"I must beat him out. It's the only way I can do anything. Go, Pink-eye! Go!" And

Pink-eye did go as he had never gone before since Tad Butler had owned him.

Slowly but surely he was heading off the other horse. They saw him now and a few scattering shots were sent in his direction, but the lad heeded them no more than had they been rain drops. His mind was too fully absorbed with the task he had set for himself.

At last he and the rancher's pony were converging on a single point. Mr. Simms's pony reached it first with Tad only a few feet away. They were fairly between the lines now and bullets were flying about them. Tad could hear their whut! whut! as they sped past him.

He had lost the race. But there still remained one more resource. His rope was in its place. Tad slipped it from the saddle horn and made a quick reach for the rancher.

He groaned when he saw that he had missed his aim.

Yet, instead of giving up the battle, the lad was more determined than ever to rescue the owner of the herd that he had cast his fortunes with. The rowels were dug into the sides of the pony with a firmer pressure than before, and Tad began rapidly to haul in the lariat with one hand. When once he felt the knot at his finger tips he began whirling the loop over his head, leaning well forward in his saddle, riding at a tremendous pace on the fleet-footed little pony.

He cast. This time the loop fell true.

"Steady! steady! Pink-eye," he cautioned, taking a quick turn about the pommel. To stop too suddenly might throw the other pony on its side and crush the rancher.

The lariat had dropped over the other animal's neck and was quickly drawn down. Pinkeye stopped, braced himself as he felt his fellow slowing down under the pressure of the loop on his neck.

"Whoa!" commanded Tad sharply, leaping from the saddle and taking up on the lariat as fast as he could.

A shrill yell from the cowmen told him they would be upon him in a moment. They understood now what he was trying to do.

Tad worked with feverish haste to release Mr. Simms from the stirrups. Yet when he had finally accomplished this, his work was not yet half done. He did not know whether the rancher was dead or alive, nor had he the time to satisfy himself on this point.

Grasping Mr. Simms under the arms, the lad dragged him over to Pink-eye, and with a strength born of the excitement of the moment, succeeded in throwing the rancher's body over the back of his own pony.

The lad was panting in short, quick breaths. He had barely enough strength left to crawl on Pink-eye's back. Once there, he fairly fell across Mr. Simms's body, clinging to it with one hand, the other gripped on the pommel.

Pink-eye seemed to know what was expected of him, for straightway he got under motion, trotting off toward the lines of the sheepmen.

The cowboys turned their guns on the little outfit, but the sheepmen now discovering what was going on, gave a mighty yell and swept down on their enemy.

The cowboys gave way before the resistless rush, and whirling their ponies, raced for the foothills, with the pursuers shooting and yelling as they lashed and spurred their ponies after them.

Tad was almost overwhelmed as the sheepmen rushed by him. But he had saved Mr. Simms and he did not care if the jostling ponies of his friends had almost run him down in their mad rush.

The lad now gaining in strength, pulled himself to a sitting posture and hurried Pink-eye along at a little faster gait. They were headed for the camp, which they reached in a few minutes.

Tenderly the lad lifted the rancher from the saddle, stretching him out on the grass. His first care was to determine whether the man were alive or dead.

"He's alive!" cried Tad exultingly. "He's only stunned."

A bullet had grazed the rancher's head, ploughing a little furrow as it passed, but there was nothing more. Had Tad not reached him in time no doubt he would have been killed.

Getting water from the chuck wagon, Tad bathed the wound and dashed water into the rancher's face until signs of returning consciousness were evident. After a little while Mr. Simms opened his eyes and asked what had happened.

Tad told him, leaving out his own part in the rescue entirely, save that he had brought him in.

The lad, after telling Mr. Simms that the cowboys had been driven off, helped the rancher to his tent and put him to bed, or rather induced him to lie down on his cot, for Mr. Simms's head was whirling.

No sooner had Tad done this than he heard a galloping pony rapidly approaching the camp. The lad stepped out as the horseman pulled up. It was the foreman. He threw himself from his mount and started on a run for Mr. Simms's tent.

"Hello!" he exclaimed, bringing up short. "Where's the boss? Is he hurt? What happened to him?" he demanded excitedly, without giving Tad a chance to answer between questions.

"I think he is all right, Mr. Larue. He had a close call" --

"Was he shot?"

"A bullet grazed the side of his head, and then his pony ran away. I guess that came nearer killing him than did the bullet."

"He owes his life to you, and that's no joke," answered the foreman shortly. "We didn't see that he was in trouble till one of the boys discovered you chasing his pony. Then we saw you rope the critter and pack the boss on your own cayuse."

"Was - was anybody killed?" asked Tad hesitatingly.

"No. Mary got a bullet through the calf of his right leg, and Bat Coyne lost a piece of an ear. Guess that's about all."

"Yes; but what of the others? Were any of the cowmen killed?"

"No such luck," growled the foreman. "We pinked a few of them, but they're too tough to kill. We come mighty near having a fight, however," he mused.

"Near!" exploded the boy. "I should say. you were right up to it."

"We've lost a lot of sheep, boy; that's of more consequence."

"How many?"

"No telling. Can't tell till morning. It'll take all day to round up the scattered bunches - those that were not killed."

"Where are the boys - Ned and the rest of them?" asked Tad, suddenly bethinking himself of his companions.

"Oh, that's what I came back here for - one of the things. They're all right. That is, they're out there with the bunch, except Phil. Have you seen him?"

"Phil? No. Where is he?"

"He was with me, but he got away somewhere."

"Phil gone?"

"It seems so."

"Oh, that's too bad. What shall we do?"

"Go hunt for him. Do you want to join me?" asked the foreman, with sudden energy, leaping into his saddle again.

"Of course I do," answered Tad Butler, running for his own pony and following the foreman out of camp at a quick gallop.

CHAPTER XXI

TWO BOYS STRANGELY MISSING

"No use. He's been picked up by those dastardly cowmen," growled Luke after he and Tad had searched until daybreak. "We must go back to the camp and then turn out the outfit. We've got to find him, that's all. Mr. Simms will be crazy when he hears that the boy has strayed away from us."

"What do you think he'll do?" asked Tad in a worried tone.

"Heaven only knows. If it's those cow fellows who have done it, he'll never rest till he's settled with them for good and all. I'll plan out a hunt for the kid, but it has got to be each man for himself. We must cover every inch of the territory to the north, west and south of us. He couldn't have gone the other way. Come, let's be hustling back to camp."

"Perhaps they have not taken him at all. I should not be surprised if he were only lost."

But Luke shook his head. He was convinced that the rancher's son had not strayed away of his own accord. He believed that the cowmen had picked the lad up and carried him away for sheer revenge on Mr. Simms.

Having seen Philip at Groveland Comers, some of them knew him, argued the foreman.

When Mr. Simms was informed of the loss of Phil, he was well-nigh beside himself.

"Do something! Why don't you do something?" he exclaimed in agony.

"We have," answered Luke. "And we have returned to get the rest of your men started on a daylight hunt."

"Did he take his pony with him?" asked Tad, as a thought occurred to him.

"Yes," replied Luke.

"Then, if the pony has not come back, it is pretty good evidence that Philip is still on his back, it seems to me."

"Then turn out; everybody turn out!" shouted Mr. Simms. "Don't come back till you get him or bring me some tidings."

"You will want some one to round up each scattered band of sheep, Mr. Simms. You do not want to lose your herd, do you?" asked the foreman.

"I don't care for the herd. Let two men and the dogs remain with the sheep that did not stampede. All the rest go out on the search. I'll take a turn myself. What's your plan, Luke?"

The foreman explained that he proposed to send the searchers out alone, so that all the territory might be covered. He had planned to lay his party out in the shape of a fan. The fan closed, he would push up into the foothills, then open it in a wide sweep. As he expressed it, "not even a jack rabbit could get away from them if he were within the semicircle covered by their formation."

Mr. Simms bore the strain as well as a father could be expected to bear it.

Without the loss of a moment Luke gathered the men about him, explaining briefly what was to be done and assigning to each man the part he was to play in the day's search.

Foremost among the party were the Pony Rider Boys. Even Stacy Brown, serious-faced and impatient to be off, had saddled and bridled his pony and sat awaiting the order to move.

At last all was ready.

"Right!" announced the foreman, whereupon the sheepmen, headed by Luke and Tad Butler, started up at a brisk gallop, headed straight across the mesa, taking a course that would lead them to the foothills, a short distance ahead of them. Beaching the foothills, they continued on for some two or three miles. Here the foreman gave the order to open the fan, he taking the lead on the left and Tad on the right. The searchers were now moving with a space of about a quarter of a mile between them,

shouting out the name of Phil Simms now and then, these calls running down the line to the lower end of the fan-shaped formation.

After a time Tad found that he could no longer hear the shouts of his companions, yet from the position of the sun, which he consulted frequently, he felt sure that he was following the right course.

On and on he rode, until the sun lay on the western horizon. The others of the party were making a thorough search, investigating every gully and draw that lay in their course, shouting for Phil, hut not shooting their guns, as this was to be the signal that the lost boy had been found.

"I'm afraid we are going to miss him," mused the foreman. "If we fail to find him, then they've got him, sure."

At last he had completed his half of the sweep of the fan, and his face wore a troubled look as his pony emerged from the foothills onto the open mesa again. The sun was setting.

Luke rode out and waited a few moments, and when joined by the rest of his section, started back to the camp.

Old Hicks had prepared the hated mutton for supper by the time the right side of the fan formation got in. Not a trace had one of them found of the missing Philip Simms.

The rancher said nothing when told that they had failed. He strode away to his tent and they saw him no more for hours.

They had just gathered about the table for the evening meal, all unusually silent, when Ned Rector, glancing about, made a sudden discovery.

"Where's Tad?" he demanded.

"Didn't he come in?" asked the foreman, pausing in the act of sitting down to the table.

"That's what I should like to know? Where is he?"

No one seemed to know.

"Now, he's gone, too," breathed the foreman anxiously. "That's one more mystery on the old Custer trail."

"We - we'll have to go hunt for Tad now. You don't suppose he and Phil are together, do you?" asked Walter.

"I don't know. I hope they are. But, boy, it's useless to go out looking for them now. All we can do will be to wait until morning, then take up the search again" --

"That's what comes from taking kids out on a man's job," growled Old Hicks, as he served the mutton.

"Hicks, no one asked you for your opinion," snapped the foreman. "These boys have done men's work ever since they joined. Had it not been for Tad, Boss Simms would have been out of business entirely now. Don't let me hear anybody casting any slurs on these boys. I won't stand for it."

Old Hicks grumbled and hobbled away to his black kettle, while the others ate their supper in silence. But, somehow, the meal was far from satisfying, and one by one they rose from the table, leaving plates half filled, and strolled away to spend the evening as best they could until bedtime. Ned and the foreman remained up, for they were to go out at midnight and take their trick at watching over the herd.

"I've just got an idea," said the foreman, calling Ned to him.

"Yes; what is it?"

"I'm going to put some one on the herd in my place and ride over to Groveland. Want to go along?"

"Yes, if it has anything to do with our friends."

"That's what I mean."

"All right, I'm ready; but it is pretty late."

"Makes no difference. We'll wake them up if they are in bed. I want to see Cavanagh, who keeps the store. I have one or two questions to ask him."

Without saying anything to the others as to their intention, the two quietly saddled their ponies and rode off. The foreman made arrangements to have others take their trick, after which they headed across the mesa toward the place where Tad had whipped the mountain boy.

Though the night, like the one that had preceded it, was intensely dark, Luke rode on with perfect confidence, never for one instant hesitating over the course.

Ned did not know that they had reached the little

village until the foreman told him.

"We're here," he said quietly.

"Where's the town?"

"In it now."

"I don't see it, if we are."

"You hold my horse. I'll wake up Cavanagh," announced the foreman, dismounting and tossing the reins to his companion.

Luke thundered on the front door of the store, above which the owner had his quarters. After an interval, during which the foreman had pounded insistently with the butt of his revolver, an upper window opened and a voice demanded to know what was wanted.

"Come down here and I'll tell you."

"Who are you? What do you mean prowling around this time of the night?"

"I'm Luke Larue, of the Simms's outfit, and I want to see you."

"Oh, hello, Luke. Thought there was something familiar about your voice. I'll be down in a minute. Anybody with you?" "Yes, friend. Hurry up." Cavanagh opened the front door, peering out suspiciously before he permitted his caller to enter.

"Wait a minute. I want to call my friend in. Ned, tether the ponies and come along."

After the lad had joined them, the two ranchers entered the store, the proprietor taking them to the back of the store and lighting a lantern, which he placed behind a cracker barrel, so that the light might not be observed from the outside,

"Now, what is it?" he demanded. Luke told him briefly of the battle with the cowboys, of which Cavanagh had already heard. Then he related the story of the mysterious disappearance of the two boys.

"What do you want of me?" asked the storekeeper, when the story had been finished.

"To know whether you had heard any of the boys say anything that might lead you to believe they knew anything about the matter?"

"No," answered Canavagh after a moment's thought. "Hain't heard a word. Don't believe they know anything about it. They'd a said something if they'd heard of it."

"Don't you know anything about the boys yourself?"

"No, don't know nothing about them."

"Sure?"

"Surest thing, you know."

"Very well. I believe you. One of my reasons for coming over here, however, was to tell you to keep your eyes and ears open to-morrow."

"I'll do that for you -- "

"If we fail to find them to-morrow, I'll ride over at night after the crowd has left here and hear what you have learned. When any of the cowmen come in, I want you to bring up the subject and try to draw them out. You'll get something that will be of use to us, I know, for I'm dead certain that they've got both of those boys."

"Do you think they would dare do a thing like that?" asked Ned.

"Dare?" Luke laughed harshly. "They'd dare anything, especially about this time. Oh, did you hear whether any of them got hit last night!"

"Two or three is laid up for repairs," grinned the storekeeper.

"I'm glad of it. I wish the whole bunch had been trimmed."

"Lose many sheep?"

"Yes; too many. But that isn't what's troubling us now."

"No, I understand. It's the kids."

"Exactly. Don't forget what you have got to do, now."

Ned had been leaning against the counter listening to the conversation, when his hand came in contact with a soft object that lay on the counter. He carelessly picked it up and looked at it.

What he had found was a sombrero. This of itself was

unimportant, for the store carried them for sale. A broad, yellow band about it was what attracted Ned Rector's attention, causing him to utter a sharp exclamation.

"What is it?" demanded Luke quickly.

"Look. Did you ever see this before?" he asked excitedly.

"It's Philip Simms's hat," answered the foreman, fixing a stern eye on the old storekeeper.

CHAPTER XXII

CAPTURED BY THE INDIANS

"Yes. I recognized it the instant I saw it," answered Ned.

"Cavanagh, what does this mean?" demanded the foreman. "I think it's up to you to explain and mighty quick at that."

"I - I don't know anything about it," stammered the storekeeper.

"Where did you get that hat?"

"I bought it."

"Off whom?"

"Don't know what his name is. I never seen him before."

"Tell me all you know. Come, I've no time to fool away asking you questions. Get to the point."

"I'll tell you all I know. A fellow came in here this afternoon. I give him fifty cents for the hat and that's all there was to it."

"Say where he come from?"

"Yes, said he was down from the Medicine range."

"That's more than thirty miles north of here," mused the foreman. "I don't understand it. You sure that's all he said?"

"Yes; I don't know any more."

"Then we'll be off. I guess we'd better hit the trail for the Medicine range to-night so as to be well on our way by daylight."

"Here's fifty cents. I'll take the hat with me," said Ned, tossing a half dollar on the counter, and stowing the sombrero under his belt.

They hurried from the store, with a parting injunction to Cavanagh to be watchful. Mounting their ponies they rode swiftly away.

"We'll return to camp before we leave for the north," said Luke.

As the sun went down, Tad, becoming concerned for himself, turned sharply to the right, urging his pony on so as to get back to camp before night. He did not relish the idea of spending another night alone in the mountains.

"I believe I don't know where I am," decided the lad at last, pulling up sharply and gazing first at the sky, then at the unfamiliar landscape about him. "I seem to have acquired the habit of getting lost. Hello, I hear some one coming. W-h-o-o-p-e-e!" he shouted to attract the attention of the newcomers, hoping that it might be some of the men from the Simms outfit.

There were several of them, and though they made no reply, he heard them turn their ponies in his direction. Suddenly there rode into the little clearing where he was sitting on his pony, half a dozen men, the sight of whom made him take a short, sharp breath.

"Indians!" he gasped.

With gaudily painted faces, bright blankets and buckskin suits, they made a picturesque group as they halted and surveyed the young man questioningly.

One who appeared to be the leader of the party rode forward and peered into Tad's face.

"How," he grunted.

"How," answered Tad, saluting bravely, but feeling far from brave at that moment.

A second and younger brave rode up at this point and in very good English asked the lad who he was.

"I am from the Simms sheep ranch, and I guess I have lost my way. If you can set me straight, I shall be very much obliged."

The younger man consulted with the older one, who had greeted Tad first.

"The chief says we are going that way. If you will come along with us we will leave you within about a mile of the camp."

"Very well," answered the boy, with some reluctance. They seemed friendly enough and, besides, there could be no danger to him in accompanying them.

As they started to move on, Tad clucked to Pink-eye and fell in with the party. He noticed shortly, that the others had ridden up and that he was in reality surrounded by the painted braves. Then he remembered that he had heard of roving bands of Indians in that part of the country - Indians who had been getting off their reservations and indulging in various depredations.

"Are we getting near the place?" asked the lad finally, a growing uneasiness rising within him.

"I'll ask the chief," said the young Indian, who had been riding by Tad's side. "He says it will he two hours yet," was the reply, after a series of grunts and gestures had passed between the men.

"It didn't take me that long to get here."

"Camp almost one sun away."

"Who is he?" indicating the leader of the party.

"Chief."

"What's his name?"

"Chief Willy. He doesn't talk much English."

"You do, though," answered Tad, glancing up at the expressionless face of his companion.

"Me with Wild West show long, long time."

"Is that so. Maybe I have seen you. Were you with the show that was in Chillicothe last summer? I saw the show then."

"Me with um," answered the redskin.

"Why, that's interesting," said the boy, now thoroughly interested and for the time so absorbed in questioning the Indian about his life with the show that he forgot his own uneasiness.

By this time, darkness intense and impenetrable, at least to the eyes of the boy, had settled down about them. Yet it seemed to make no difference to the Indians, who kept their ponies at a steady jog-trot, picking their way unerringly, avoiding rocks and treacherous holes as if it were broad daylight.

Tad did not try to guide Pink-eye any more, but let him follow the others, and when he got a little out of his course, the pony next to him would crowd Pink-eye over where he belonged.

"Seems to me we are a long time getting there," announced the boy finally. He was beginning to grow uneasy again.

"Come camp bymeby," informed the young Indian. "Chief, him know way."

Tad had his doubts about that, but he thought it best not to tell them of his misgivings until he was certain. Perhaps they were honest Indians after all and were only seeking to do him a favor.

The lad was getting tired and hungry, having had nothing more than a mutton sandwich since early morning. He judged it must be getting close to midnight now.

As if interpreting his thoughts, the young Indian rode up close beside him, at the same time thrusting something into Tad's hand. "What is it?" asked the boy. "Eat. Good meat," answered the Indian. The boy nibbled at it gingerly. It was meat of some kind, and it was tough. But most anything in the nature of food was acceptable to him then, so he helped himself more liberally and enjoyed his lunch. The dried meat was excellent, even if it was tough to chew.

After a little they came to a level stretch, and now the Indians put their ponies to a lively gallop, which Pink-eye, being surrounded by the other ponies, was forced to fall into to keep from getting run down by the riders behind him. Faster and faster they forced their mounts forward, uttering sharp little exclamations to urge them on, accompanied by sundry grunts and unintelligible mutterings.

That they all meant something, the boy felt sure. But it meant nothing to him so far as understanding was concerned.

After hours had passed the lad found all at once that the gray dawn was upon them and it was not many minutes before the stolid faces of his companions stood out clear and distinct.

Tad jerked Pink-eye up sharply.

"See here, where are you taking me to?" he demanded.

"Camp," grunted the young Indian.

"You're not. You are taking me away. I shall not go another step with you."

Summoning all his courage the boy turned his pony about and started to move away. A quick, grunted order from the chief and one of the braves caught Pink-eye's bridle, jerking him back to his previous position.

"Take your hands off, please," demanded Tad quietly. "You've no right to do that. For some reason you have deceived me and taken me far from home. I'll -- "

"No make chief angry," urged the young brave.

"I tell you I'm going. You let me alone," persisted the boy, making another effort to ride from them.

This time the chief whirled his own pony across Tad's path. From under his blanket, he permitted the boy to see the muzzle of a revolver that was protruding there.

"Ugh!" grunted the chief. "Him say you must go. Him shoot! No hurt paleface boy."

Tad hesitated. His inclination was to put spurs to Pink-eye and dash away. He did not fear the chief's revolver so much for himself. He did fear, however, that the chief might shoot his pony from under him, which would leave the boy in a worse predicament still.

"All right, I'll go with you. But I warn you the first white man I see, I'll tell him you are taking me away."

"Ugh!"

"If he shoots, I don't see how he can help hurting me," added the lad to himself, with a mirthless grin.

"Bymeby, boy go back with paleface friends."

"That's what I expect to do. But if Luke Larue finds out you have taken me away against my will, he'll do some shooting before the big chief gets a chance to. Where are you taking me to?"

Shrugs of the shoulders was all the answer that Tad could get, so he decided to make the best of his position and escape at the first opportunity. Keeping his eyes on the alert he followed along without further protest.

Once, as they ascended a sudden rise of ground on the gallop, he discovered two horsemen on beyond them about half a mile as near as he was able to judge.

Evidently the Indians saw them at the same instant, for they changed their course and went off into the rougher lands to the left.

"Had they been nearer, I'd have taken a chance and yelled for help," thought the boy. "I will do it the next time I get a chance even if they are a long way off. I can make somebody hear."

But they gave him no chance to put his plan into practice. Not a human being did Tad see during the rest of the journey, nor even a sign of human habitation. Evidently they were traveling through a very rough, uninhabited part of the state. If this were the case, he reasoned that they must be working northward. This surmise was verified with the rising of the sun.

Chief Willy gave the lad a quick glance and grunted when he saw his captive looking up at the sun.

The chief then uttered a series of grunts, which the younger Indian interpreted as meaning that they would soon reach their destination.

Tad was somewhat relieved to hear this, for he ached all over from his many hours in the saddle. Then again he was sleepy and hungry as well. They offered him no more food, so he concluded that they had none. In any event he did not propose to ask for more, even if he were starving.

Along about nine o'clock in the morning they came suddenly upon a broad river. Without hesitation the braves plunged their ponies in, with Tad and Pink-eye following. There was nothing else they could do tinder the circumstances.

The water was not deep, however, the chief having chosen a spot for fording where the stream was not above the ponies' hips. Tad lifted up his legs to keep them dry, but the Indians stolidly held their feet in their stirrups, appearing not to notice that they were getting wet.

"What river is this!" he asked, the first question he had ventured in a long time.

The young brave referred the question to his chief, to which the usual grunt of response was made.

"Him say don't know."

Tad grinned.

"For men who can find their way in the dark as well as these fellows can, they know less than I would naturally suppose," smiled the boy.

The chief saw the smile and scowled.

Tad made careful note of the fording place in case he should have occasion to cross the river on his own hook later on. He examined the hills on both sides of the stream at the same time.

Leaving the river behind them, they began a gradual ascent. Now they did not seem to be in so great a hurry as before, and allowed their ponies to walk for a mile or so, after which they took up their easy jog again. Shortly after that the boy descried several wreaths of smoke curling up into the morning sky. The Indians were heading straight toward the smoke.

At first Tad had felt a thrill of hope. But a few moments later when a number of tepees grew slowly out of the landscape he saw that they were approaching what appeared to be an Indian village, and his heart sank within him.

CHAPTER XXIII

IN THE HOME OF THE BLACKFEET

Their coming was greeted by the loud barking of dogs, while from the tepees appeared as if by magic, women and children, together with innumerable braves and boys.

They fairly swarmed out into the open space in front of the camp, setting up a shout as they recognized the newcomers.

"They seem to be mighty glad to see us,"

growled Tad. "Wish I could say as much for them."

The ponies, seeming to share the general good feeling, pricked up their ears and dashed into the camp at a gallop, Pink-eye with the rest. Almost before the little animals had come to a stop, the braves threw themselves from their saddles and darted into their tepees.

"They seem to have left me out of it, so I guess I'll go back," decided the lad half humorously. But he was given no chance to slip away. The young brave who had accompanied his chief, came running out and grasped the pony by its bridle.

"Boy, git off," he said.

Tad threw a leg over the pommel and landed on the ground. He could hardly stand, so stiff were his legs.

The young brave took him into one of the tepees, held the flap aside while Tad entered, then closed it. The lad heard him moving away. Tired out and dispirited, Tad Butler threw himself down on the grass and, in spite of his troubles, was asleep in a few moments.

A dog barking in front of his tepee awakened him. The boy pulled the flap aside ever so little and peered out. He was surprised to find that the sun was setting. He had been asleep practically all day long.

Scrambling to his feet hastily the lad stepped outside. He did not know whether he would be permitted to roam about, but he proposed to try. The answer came quickly. A brave whom he had not seen before suddenly appeared and, with a grunt of disapproval, grabbed Tad by the arms, fairly flinging him into the tepee.

The lad's cheeks burned with indignation.

"I'll teach them to insult me like that," he fumed, shaking his fist toward the opening. "I'll look out anyway."

He did so, prudently drawing the flap close whenever he heard anyone approaching. Once as he peered out, a disreputable looking cur snapped at his legs. First, the lad coaxed the animal, then tried to drive him away, finally administering a kick that sent the dog away howling.

"I've got revenge on one of the gang anyway," he laughed. "But it's not much of a revenge, at that. I wonder if they are going to bring me anything to eat. I -- "

The flap was suddenly jerked aside and the face of the chief appeared in the opening.

"How," greeted Chief Willy.

"How," answered Tad rather sullenly. "What do you want?"

"Paleface want eat?"

"You ought not to have to ask that question. So you can talk English just a little bit? Chief, when are you going to let me go away from here? It will only get you into trouble if you try to keep me. They are sure to find me."

"No find," grunted the chief.

"Oh, yes they will."

"Ugh," answered the redskin, hastily withdrawing. Then followed another long period when Tad was left alone with his thoughts.

"I wonder two things," thought the lad aloud. "I wonder what he brought me here for and I wonder when I am going to get something to eat? Captured by the Indians, eh? That's more than the rest of the Pony Riders can say."

Yet there was a more serious side to it all. They had

taken him prisoner for some purpose, but what that purpose was he could not imagine.

His thoughts were interrupted by some one silently entering the tent. Glancing up, Tad saw a slender, rather pretty Indian girl standing there looking down at him.

The boy scrambled to his feet and took off his sombrero.

"How," he said.

The girl answered in kind. Then she placed on the ground before him a bowl of soup and a plate of steaming stew. Tad sniffed the odor of mutton, which now was so familiar to him, wondering at the same time, if it had come from Mr. Simms's flock.

"Thank you," he said. "If you will excuse me I will eat. I'm awfully hungry.

She nodded and Tad went at the meal almost ravenously. The Indian girl squatted down on the ground and watched him.

"What's your name?" he asked between mouthfuls.

"Jinny."

"That's a funny name. Doesn't sound like an Indian name. Is it?"

"Me not know. Young buck heap big eat," she added.

"Yes. Oh, yes, I have something of an appetite,"

laughed Tad. "Jinny, what are they going to do with me, do you know?"

The girl shook her head with emphasis.

"What tribe is this?"

"Blackfeet. Other paleface boy here too."

Tad set down his plate and surveyed her inquiringly.

"Say that again, please. You say there's another paleface boy here in this village?"

Jinny nodded vigorously.

"Who is he?"

"Jinny not know."

"When did he - how long has he been here?"

"Sun-up."

"This morning?"

"Yes. He there," pointing with a finger to the lower end of the village.

Tad's curiosity was aroused. He wondered if another besides himself had been made an unwilling guest by the Blackfeet wanderers. If so, it must have been by another party. A sudden thought occurred to him. Tad was wearing a cheap ring on the little finger of his left hand. He had picked up the ring on the plains in Texas. Hastily stripping it from his finger he handed it to the girl.

"Want it, Jinny?"

She did. Her eyes sparkled as she slipped it on her own finger and held it off to view the effect.

"Thank," she said, turning her glowing eyes on Tad.

"You're welcome. But now I want you to do something for me. I'll send you another, a big, big ring when I get home, if you will help me to get away from here."

Jinny eyed him steadily for a few seconds, then shook her head.

"I'll send you beads, too, Jinny - beads like the paleface ladies wear."

"You send Jinny white woman beads!"

"I promise you."

"Me help um little paleface buck. Me help um two," she added, holding up two fingers. Without another word, she slipped from the tepee as silently as she had come.

Tad pondered over this last remark for some time. He did not understand what Jinny had meant.

"So I'm a buck, am I? That's one thing I haven't been called before since I have been out on the range. She said she would help me to get away. I wonder when she is going to do it."

Though Tad waited patiently until late in the evening, he saw no more of the little Indian girl. Shortly after dark several camp-fires were lighted, the cheerful blazes lighting up the street or common in front of the row of tepees in which his own was located.

Children played about the fires, the dogs were disputing over the bones tossed to them after the evening meal, while the squaws and braves, gathered in separate groups, were squatting about, gesticulating and talking.

To Tad Butler the scene held a real interest. He had never before seen an Indian camp, and least of all been a prisoner in it. He lay down on his stomach, with elbows on the ground, chin in hands, and gazed out over the village curiously.

"I wonder who that other boy is," he mused. "I presume he is a prisoner, too. Hello, there's my guard."

An Indian, with knees clasped in his arms, was rocking to and fro a little distance from the tepee. Though he was not looking toward Tad's tent, the lad felt sure the fellow had been placed there to watch him. He understood then why Jinny had not been to the tepee since bringing his meal.

Finally the camp quieted down, the fires smouldered and the dogs stretched out before them for sleep. Tad Butler's tired head drooped lower and lower, his elbows settling until his arms were down and he was lying prone upon the ground, sound asleep.

After a time the Indian whom the lad had seen sitting out in front rose, and, stepping softly to the tepee, looked in. He gave a grunt of satisfaction, threw himself down right at the entrance and was snoring heavily half a minute later.

The camp slumbered on undisturbed until aroused by the ill-natured curs at daybreak next morning.

Tad was awakened by one of them barking at his door and snapping at him. Suddenly pulling his flap open, he hurled his sombrero in the dog's face, frightening it, so that it slunk away with a howl. Tad, laughing heartily, reached out and recovered the hat.

"Hey, there, I want to wash," he called to a brave who was passing. The redskin paid no attention to him. "All right, if you won't, then I'll go without you."

He stepped boldly from the tepee and headed for a small stream at the left of the village, which he had observed on the previous day. He had not gone far before he observed that he was being followed at a distance. He did not let it appear that he noticed this, and after making his toilet strolled back to his tepee.

Tad shrewdly reasoned that if he could induce them to relax their vigilance over him, he would have a better chance to make his escape, and he determined that he would act as if he had no intention of leaving.

He made an effort to find out where they had tethered Pink-eye, but there were no signs of ponies anywhere. He knew, however, that they could not be far away, for the Indian always keeps in touch with his mount.

Jinny came with his breakfast at sunrise. He noticed the first thing that she was not wearing the ring he had given her, but before he had an opportunity to comment on it, the girl drew the ring from a pocket, placed it on a finger and fell to admiring it.

Tad laughed and turned to his breakfast. This consisted of a big bowl of corn meal, steaming hot, with some cold mutton on the side. Frankly, he admitted to himself that he had eaten far worse meals in more civilized communities.

"Good morning, Jinny. I was so much interested in the breakfast that I forgot to say it when you first came in. This is very good. Did you cook it?"

She nodded.

"I thought so. You beat Old Hicks's cooking already. Hicks is the cook out on Mr. Simms's sheep ranch, where I come from. Understand?"

"Yes."

"I thought you were going to help me to escape," said Tad, suddenly leaning toward her. "Aren't you?"

Jinny made a sign for silence, and then went to the opening and peered out cautiously. She returned, and, placing her mouth close to the lad's ear, whispered, "Byrneby."

Tad could scarcely repress a laugh at the tragic tone in which she said it. Yet his face was perfectly sober and he continued with his breakfast without further comment.

Jinny gathered up the dishes and left him without a

word. After a time the boy pulled back the flaps and sat down to watch the life of the camp by daylight. The squaws were busily at work, carrying wood and engaged in other occupations, though few of the braves were to be seen. The boy concluded that they must be sleeping.

The hours dragged along slowly. It seemed an age until night came once more. Somehow he felt that the night would bring him good luck. A warning glance from the Indian girl when she brought his supper told him that conversation were better not indulged in, so he said nothing to her. She left the dishes with him and went away at once.

That night Tad sat up until late, hoping vainly for word from Jinny, but none came. When the guard approached the tent along toward midnight, Tad feigned sleep, and so well did he feign it that he really went to sleep.

He thought he had been napping but a few moments, when a peculiar scratching sound on the back of his tepee brought him up sitting, every nerve on the alert.

Tad peered out through the flap. The guard was asleep. He crept back to the other side of the tepee and scratched on the tepee wall with his finger-nail.

"S-h-h."

The warning was accompanied by a slight ripping sound, and he knew the wall was being slit with a knife.

"Paleface buck, come with Jinny," whispered a voice in his ear.

CHAPTER XXIV

CONCLUSION

Grasping the lad by the arm, the Indian girl led him cautiously straight back from the tepee, guiding him in the darkness unerringly, around all obstructions.

After proceeding in a straight line for some distance, she turned and made a wide detour around the camp. He could tell this by the light of the smouldering camp-fires. He dared ask no questions until Jinny had given him permission to speak, which was not until they had left the camp some distance behind them. She paused suddenly and faced him.

"You send Jinny ring?"

"Yes, I promised you."

"You send beads like white women wear?"

"Of course I will."

"Then come. Ponies here. Boy here."

Not understanding her latter words, Tad followed obediently, passing around a point of rocks.

"Here ponies. Here boy."

"O Tad, is that you?" exclaimed a tremulous voice.

"Who's that?" demanded Tad sharply.

"It's Phil. O Tad!"

"Phil!" cried the lad, grasping the boy about the neck and hugging him delightedly. "They got you too, did they? Oh, I'm so glad I've found you! You must tell me all about it, hut not now. We've got to get away from here. Thank you, Jinny. I shall never forget this. *I*"

"You send Jinny beads?" demanded the girl suggestively.

"Indeed you shall have the finest set of beads that an Indian girl ever wore, even if it takes all my money to buy them. Now which way shall we go?"

"Go river."

"Where is it?"

She took his hand in the darkness and pointed with it in the direction where the river lay.

"Yes, yes, I know. Then where?"

"Find white man. He tell um. Jinny not know."

She pressed something into his hand.

"What's this?" asked Tad sharply.

"Knife. Mebbyso brave catch um paleface buck."

Tad caught the significance of her words instantly.

"No, Jinny, thank you very much. I couldn't do that. You keep the knife. I shall not need it, but you shall have the beads just the same."

"Ugh! Go pony. Go quick. Braves him follow." She pointed back toward the camp, and, grasping Tad by the arm, hurried him toward the ponies.

"When?"

"Come now," she insisted.

Tad felt a sudden thrill as he heard a great commotion back in the camp.

"We've got to hurry, Phil. I guess they have discovered our escape. You run, Jinny. Run back. Don't you let them know you helped us. Say, what will the chief do if he finds it out?" demanded the boy, pausing sharply.

"Huh. Jinny no afraid chief. Jinny laugh in chief face. Bye."

She disappeared with surprising suddenness.

"Quick, Phil! Get on your pony and follow me. Keep close to me."

"I am on," answered the boy bravely. "It's my pony, too."

"And so is this one mine. It's Pink-eye." "What's that

noise!" asked Phil in a tremulous voice.

"Hi-yi-yip-yah - yah-hi-yah!" rang out the Indian war cry, as the braves threw themselves on the bare backs of their ponies and tore from the village, going in all directions.

Tad drove the spurs in viciously.

"Quick! Quick, Phil! They're after us."

"I'm coming."

Both ponies sprang away in the darkness, the lads clinging to the saddles, none too sure of the path that lay before them, and riding desperately.

Bang, bang, bang!

Three rifle shots rang out in quick succession, and the boys imagined they could hear the bullets sing over their heads.

"Hi-yi-yip - yah-hi-yah!"

"They're gaining on us. They're gaining, Phil. Ride for your life!"

The shrill yells of the Indians sounded much closer. The boys believed that their enemies had picked up the trail.

"We have got to do something, and do it quick. We've got to outwit them," shouted Tad.

"What - what" --

Frank Gee Patchin

"I'll tell you. When we think they are getting too near, I'll pull over by you and take you on my pony. We'll send the other one flying on while we turn off," decided Tad.

The time for the change came a few moments later. The Indians were gaining on them every second. Now the "hi-yi-yip - yah-hi-yah" sounded as if it was being shrieked into their ears.

Tad drove Pink-eye right against the other pony.

"Jump!" he commanded, and Phil landed on Pink-eye's back without mishap, while Tad, giving a vicious kick to the free pony, turned off to the left a little and drove his pony at a run. They reached the river. As the pony plunged in the boys slipped off on opposite sides of him, hanging to the saddle while the pony swam.

"Hang on tightly. Don't let go. There is a strong current here."

They could hear the savages racing up and down the river bank, shouting and shooting and searching vainly for the other pony. Every minute Tad expected to hear them take to the river, but for some reason they did not do so. After a chilling swim, the boys at last reached the other bank, and, shaking the water from their clothes as best they could, both mounted the one pony and struck off, guided by the stars alone.

They continued on until daylight, having heard nothing more of the Indians. Both boys were shivering with cold and exhausted for want of something to eat after their trying night.

Tad learned from his companion that he had been taken by white men and turned over to the Indians for some purpose unknown to him. Phil described his captor as a man with a scar on his temple and having a red beard.

Shortly after sunrise they came upon a flock of sheep, and soon after they were at the house of a rancher, where the boys told their story. The owner of the ranch knew Mr. Simms well, and besides providing Phil with a pony, sent one of his own men to pilot the boys home.

They rode into the Simms camp about midnight, rousing the camp with their shouts. And the jollification that followed the safe return of Phil and his rescuer did the hearts of both boys good. There was no sleep in the Simms outfit that night.

Tad and Phil were obliged to tell the story of their experiences over and over again, while the other boys listened in wide-eyed wonder.

Mr. Simms was of the opinion that, having taken Phil, the Indians picked up Tad so that he might not report their being off the reservation.

"At any rate we have got the man, thanks to your description," he added.

"What, the man with the scar?"

"Yes. He is the cattle rancher whom Luke insisted was such a friend of his. I took a long chance and had the sheriff arrest him to-day. He is being held until you take a look to see if you can identify him. I hope you will be able to."

"Where is he?" asked the lad. "Tied up in the chuck wagon. I'll have him brought over."

"Hello, Bluff," greeted Tad, the instant he set eyes on the surly face of the prisoner.

"Hello, kid. Never saw me before, did you?"

"I should say I had. That's the man, Mr. Simms. There can be no doubt about it."

"And he is the fellow who caught and turned me over to the Indians," added Philip, shrinking away from the bearded face.

"Then I guess there is nothing more to he said," announced Mr. Simms, with a grim smile. "This man has been doing a crooked business for years, all up and down the trail. Of course he had accomplices, but we shall hardly get them. Nobody suspected him. The frequent thefts of stock and the killing of sheep was a mystery until you solved it, Master Tad. I wish I knew how to express my appreciation of what you have done for us."

"There is one favor you can do for me if you will, Mr. Simms."

"It is already granted. Name it."

"I wish you would see that Jinny gets the beads I promised her and which I am going to buy as soon as I get where I can."

"She shall have them," replied the rancher, "and a present from me, besides. I'll send one of my men to the Blackfeet Agency especially to deliver your present and mine to the Indian girl."

"Thank you."

"To-morrow we shall have to go back to town with the sheriff and his prisoner. I should like to have you accompany us if you will. The prosecuting attorney can take your deposition and thus avoid the necessity of your having to wait for the trial. You are free to continue on your trip then, if you desire."

"Of course he will go with you," spoke up the Professor, who, up to that point, had been too deeply absorbed in the developments of the hour to offer any comment. "All of us will accompany you. Boys, you had better get your belongings together before we turn in, as I imagine Mr. Simms will want to make an early start in the morning. I guess you are all pretty well satisfied with what you have seen of the old Custer trail."

"Yes," shouted the boys. "We've had a great time."

"At least some of us have," smiled Tad.

At Forsythe next day Tad Butler and young Philip Simms appeared against the prisoner. As the result of their positive identification and further testimony, Bluff broke down. He made a full confession, implicating others who had been concerned with him in various misdeeds along the trail, each of whom was eventually brought to justice and punished.

Their presence being no longer necessary in Forsythe, that afternoon the Pony Rider Boys boarded a sleeping car, loudly cheered by a crowd of enthusiastic ranchers and villagers, who had gathered to see them off. And there, with their four smiling faces framed in the Pullman windows, we shall take leave of the Pony Rider Boys. They will next be heard from in another volume, entitled, "THE PONY RIDER BOYS IN THE OZARKS, or the Secret of Ruby Mountain," a stirring tale of adventure and daring deeds among the Missouri mountains, in which the lads pass through many perils.

Choose from Thousands of 1stWorldLibrary Classics By

Ada Leverson
Adolphus William Ward
Aesop
Agatha Christie
Alexander Aaronsohn
Alexander Kielland
Alexandre Dumas
Alfred Gatty
Alfred Ollivant
Alice Duer Miller
Alice Turner Curtis
Alice Dunbar
Ambrose Bierce
Amelia E. Barr
Andrew Lang
Andrew McFarland Davis
Andy Adams
Anna Sewell
Annie Besant
Annie Hamilton Donnell
Annie Payson Call
Annonaymous
Anton Chekhov
Arnold Bennett
Arthur Conan Doyle
Arthur M. Winfield
Arthur Ransome
Atticus
B.H. Baden-Powell
B. M. Bower
Baroness Emmuska Orczy
Baroness Orczy
Basil King
Bayard Taylor
Ben Macomber
Bertha Muzzy Bower
Bjornstjerne Bjornson
Booth Tarkington
Boyd Cable
Bram Stoker
C. Collodi
C. E. Orr
C. M. Ingleby
Carolyn Wells
Catherine Parr Traill
Charles A. Eastman
Charles Dickens
Charles Dudley Warner
Charles Farrar Browne

Charles Ives
Charles Kingsley
Charles Klein
Charles Lathrop Pack
Charles Whibley
Charles Willing Beale
Charlotte M. Braeme
Charlotte M. Yonge
Charlotte Perkins Stetson
Clair W. Hayes
Clarence Day Jr.
Clarence E. Mulford
Clemence Housman
Confucius
Cornelis DeWitt Wilcox
Cyril Burleigh
D. H. Lawrence
Daniel Defoe
David Garnett
Don Carlos Janes
Donald Keyhoe
Dorothy Kilner
Dougan Clark
Douglas Fairbanks
E. Nesbit
E.P.Roe
E. Phillips Oppenheim
Edgar Rice Burroughs
Edith Van Dyne
Edith Wharton
Edward J. O'Biren
Edward S. Ellis
Edwin L. Arnold
Eleanor Atkins
Eliot Gregory
Elizabeth Gaskell
Elizabeth McCracken
Elizabeth Von Arnim
Ellem Key
Emerson Hough
Emily Dickinson
Enid Bagnold
Enilor Macartney Lane
Erasmus W. Jones
Ernie Howard Pie
Ethel Turner
Ethel Watts Mumford
Eugenie Foa
Eugene Wood

Evelyn Everett-green
Everard Cotes
F. H. Cheley
F. J. Cross
Federick Austin Ogg
Ferdinand Ossendowski
Francis Bacon
Francis Darwin
Frances Hodgson Burnett
Frances Parkinson Keyes
Frank Gee Patchin
Frank Harris
Frank Jewett Mather
Frank L. Packard
Frank V. Webster
Frederic Stewart Isham
Frederick Trevor Hill
Frederick Winslow Taylor
Friedrich Kerst
Friedrich Nietzsche
Fyodor Dostoyevsky
G.A. Henty
G.K. Chesterton
Gabrielle E. Jackson
Garrett P. Serviss
Gaston Leroux
George Ade
Geroge Bernard Shaw
George Durston
George Ebers
George Eliot
George MacDonald
George Meredith
George Orwell
George Tucker
George W. Cable
George Wharton James
Gertrude Atherton
Grace E. King
Grace Gallatin
Grant Allen
Guillermo A. Sherwell
Gulielma Zollinger
Gustav Flaubert
H. A. Cody
H. B. Irving
H.C. Bailey
H. G. Wells
H. H. Munro

H. Irving Hancock	James DeMille	Louisa May Alcott
H. Rider Haggard	James Joyce	Lucy Fitch Perkins
H. W. C. Davis	James Lane Allen	Lucy Maud Montgomery
Hamilton Wright Mabie	James Lane Allen	Lydia Miller Middleton
Hans Christian Andersen	James Oliver Curwood	Lyndon Orr
Harold Avery	James Oppenheim	M. Corvus
Harold McGrath	James Otis	M. H. Adams
Harriet Beecher Stowe	James R. Driscoll	Margaret E. Sangster
Harry Houidini	Jane Austen	Margaret Vandercook
Helent Hunt Jackson	Jens Peter Jacobsen	Margret Penrose
Helen Nicolay	Jerome K. Jerome	Maria Edgeworth
Hendrik Conscience	John Burroughs	Maria Thompson Daviess
Hendy David Thoreau	John Cournos	Mariano Azuela
Henri Barbusse	John F. Kennedy	Marion Polk Angellotti
Henrik Ibsen	John Gay	Mark Overton
Henry Adams	John Glasworthy	Mark Twain
Henry Ford	John Habberton	Mary Austin
Henry Frost	John Joy Bell	Mary Catherine Crowley
Henry James	John Kendrick Bangs	Mary Cole
Henry Jones Ford	John Milton	Mary Hastings Bradley
Henry Seton Merriman	John Philip Sousa	Mary Roberts Rinehart
Henry W Longfellow	Jonas Lauritz Idemil Lie	Mary Rowlandson
Herbert A. Giles	Jonathan Swift	M. Wollstonecraft Shelley
Herbert N. Casson	Joseph A. Altsheler	Maud Lindsay
Herman Hesse	Joseph Carey	Max Beerbohm
Homer	Joseph Conrad	Myra Kelly
Honore De Balzac	Joseph E. Badger Jr	Nathaniel Hawthrone
Horace Walpole	Joseph Hergesheimer	Nicolo Machiavelli
Horatio Alger Jr.	Joseph Jacobs	O. F. Walton
Howard Pyle	Julian Hawthrone	Oscar Wilde
Howard R. Garis	Julies Vernes	Owen Johnson
Hugh Lofting	Justin Huntly McCarthy	P.G. Wodehouse
Hugh Walpole	Kakuzo Okakura	Paul and Mabel Thorne
Humphry Ward	Kenneth Grahame	Paul G. Tomlinson
Ian Maclaren	Kenneth McGaffey	Paul Severing
Inez Haynes Gillmore	Kate Langley Bosher	Percy Brebner
Irving Bacheller	Kate Langley Bosher	Peter B. Kyne
Israel Abrahams	Katherine Cecil Thurston	Plato
Ivan Turgenev	Katherine Stokes	R. Derby Holmes
J.G.Austin	L. A. Abbot	R. L. Stevenson
J. Henri Fabre	L. T. Meade	R. S. Ball
J. M. Barrie	L. Frank Baum	Rabindranath Tagore
J. Macdonald Oxley	Latta Griswold	Rahul Alvares
J. S. Fletcher	Laura Lee Hope	Ralph Henry Barbour
J. S. Knowles	Laurence Housman	Ralph Waldo Emmerson
J. Storer Clouston	Leo Tolstoy	Rene Descartes
Jack London	Leonid Andreyev	Rex Beach
Jacob Abbott	Lewis Carroll	Rex E. Beach
James Allen	Lilian Bell	Richard Harding Davis
James Andrews	Lloyd Osbourne	Richard Jefferies
James Baldwin	Louis Tracy	Richard Le Gallienne

Robert Barr
Robert Frost
Robert Gordon Anderson
Robert L. Drake
Robert Lansing
Robert Lynd
Robert Michael Ballantyne
Robert W. Chambers
Rosa Nouchette Carey
Rudyard Kipling
Samuel B. Allison
Samuel Hopkins Adams
Sarah Bernhardt
Selma Lagerlof
Sherwood Anderson
Sigmund Freud
Standish O'Grady
Stanley Weyman
Stella Benson
Stephen Crane
Stewart Edward White
Stijn Streuvels
Swami Abhedananda

Swami Parmananda
T. S. Ackland
T. S. Arthur
The Princess Der Ling
Thomas A. Janvier
Thomas A Kempis
Thomas Anderton
Thomas Bailey Aldrich
Thomas Bulfinch
Thomas De Quincey
Thomas H. Huxley
Thomas Hardy
Thomas More
Thornton W. Burgess
U. S. Grant
Valentine Williams
Various Authors
Victor Appleton
Virginia Woolf
Walter Camp
Walter Scott
Washington Irving
Wilbur Lawton

Wilkie Collins
Willa Cather
Willard F. Baker
William Dean Howells
William le Queux
W. Makepeace Thackeray
William W. Walter
Winston Churchill
Yei Theodora Ozaki
Yogi Ramacharaka
Young E. Allison
Zane Grey

www.ingramcontent.com/pod-product-compliance
Lightning Source LLC
Chambersburg PA
CBHW030134180626
46812CB00002B/683